D1201470

A NEW ICE AGE

by the same author

WINTER GARDEN

A NEW ICE AGE

Robert Edric

ANDRE DEUTSCH

First published in Great Britain 1986
by André Deutsch
105 Great Russell Street, London WC1B 3LJ

British Library Cataloguing in Publication Data

Edric, Robert
A new ice age.
I. Title
823'.914[F] PR6055.D7/

ISBN 0-233-97895-X

Typeset by Inforum Ltd, Portsmouth
Printed in Great Britain by
Ebenezer Baylis and Son Ltd, Worcester

For Esther

Last night I killed Mrs Devine again. Half drunk she refers to herself as the Divine Mrs Devine. It is probably a memory of something once said to her a quarter of a century ago. She has a great number of that kind of memory. They bolster her. Against us. She says it in the same way she refers to her men as 'Gentlemen Acquaintances', sounding even more like a failed music-hall comedienne. I drew the same broad knife across her throat, plunged it once into each fallen breast, and slashed again in a zigzag over her round stomach. She wore the same tightly fitting blouse and skirt as on all the other occasions and the material tore apart to reveal what lay beneath in precisely the same way. Mr Patel pinned her shoulders with his knees and held his hands together in a prayer above her head. The two West Indians held a leg each and Mrs Patel ran around us in tight circles laughing and shrieking, leaving me uncertain whether she was condemning or encouraging what we were doing. It was a satisfying dream and I awoke from it with a real sense of achievement, of having left my mark in more ways than one.

I awoke from it in the early hours, before the winter dawn, and tried to understand why it should recur at all, and why its details should be so exact, one following the other in the same precise order. What a month ago had caused me some anxiety has become, inexplicably, one of the few small pleasures of my life. I have come to savour the dream and I know I will be disappointed when it no longer returns.

I have lived with Mrs D for nine years. She owns the house in which we all live, four or six to a floor, one on top of the other, for four storeys. She herself lives on the ground floor to the rear of the house. I live in the room directly above her. If anything of her is to be seen or heard, then I am the one who sees and hears it. It is a condition of our tenancy that she has the right of access to all our rooms at any time and for any reason. Being the nearest to her, and being what I am, I am the one she visits most often. She seldom, for instance, climbs into the attic to see the West Indians, and her visits to the Patels only occur when sufficient complaints have accumulated for her to deliver them in person, the complainants usually gathering behind her as she draws in her breath and knocks. I personally have never complained. I do not need to. The others do it often enough and their complaints about the noises or smells seldom vary. Occasionally I join the small crowd around the Patels' door, and when I catch Mr Patel's eye I signal my sympathies to him. He takes none of it seriously and has come to look upon these ineffectual legations as challenging social events. More often than not he sends his wife to stand at the chained door and shout out at us in her own language. Mrs Patel, despite her proud claim to citizenship, has not yet made the slightest attempt to learn English. As she becomes louder and more excited I imagine her husband behind the door laughing at us. Mrs Devine is invariably drawn into their trap. Nothing is ever achieved, and when the gatherings break up everyone disperses, relieved simply that they are over.

I am encouraged by the killing of Mrs Devine. It is something I shall perfect. Perhaps the Patels and the West Indians have exactly the same dream at exactly the same time. Perhaps, living in this house, there is no escape from it. Perhaps even Mrs D dreams it and considers it her punishment for all her unnecessary restrictions and impositions upon us.

I doubt it.

'Mr O. Oh, Mr O.' She almost sings it. It has become one of her jokes. I am expected to laugh or smile each time I am thus addressed. She calls me 'Mr O' for two reasons: firstly, I am convinced that she does not believe the name I gave her and the one I now use is my real one; and, secondly, because nine years ago I told her I was a writer, and she considers this form of address to be more appropriate. She invests the initial with an air of mystery and romance founded on her own misconceptions, which in turn are founded on my own.

'Yes?' My disinterested reply disappoints her; she expects me to say something like 'Looking for me, Mrs D?'

'I was just wondering. You haven't seen a stranger hanging around, someone strange-looking?'

I shake my head. The street is full of strangers and strange-looking men and women.

'Mmm.'

I am expected to enquire further, but say nothing. Once started she will say whatever she has to say regardless of any distracting turns the conversation might otherwise take. Whatever it is, she will insist on coming into my room. She tries to see behind me and I shuffle from side to side, knowing that any attempt to refuse her entry will be unsuccessful.

'You can never be too careful. And with you looking out over the back garden . . .'

She pushed past me, went to the rear window and drew back the curtain. She studied the strip of land we all still referred to as the garden and then moved into the centre of the room and shook her head. I stood at the window, looking down.

'Mr Farouk said he'd seen a strange-looking man down there. Said he was looking up at the house.'

'Farouk is always seeing strange-looking men one way or another.'

'All the same . . .'

Farouk himself stands for hours looking up at the house, at his own third-storey back window. He has lived in this country for twelve years and has recently become convinced that someone is following him. Mrs D does not care what happens to him, just that it does not happen to him in her house.

She lit a cigarette and offered one to me. I accepted, knowing that by doing so she would remain for at least an hour. She relaxed, recrossed the small room and drew back the curtain on the opposite window.

'You keep it too dark,' she said. 'You should let more light in. Don't you like light?'

I told her that I found it restful in the dark, that it helped me to compose.

'Is that what you were doing then, composing?'

I admitted that I had been doing nothing prior to her arrival. She understood it to mean that I would be glad of her company.

'You get on with Mr Farouk?' she asked suspiciously. I said that he seemed friendly enough. She watched me closely. There were right answers and wrong answers.

Farouk, in addition to his persecution complex, has a fondness for Arab youths, whom he invites back to his room, leading them up the fire escape and past my own window. I wondered if Mrs D had even the faintest idea. She suspects everyone, but reserves her gravest doubts for the foreigners of which the household is largely composed. It is the reason she spends so much time with me, the reason she makes allowances. She has little sympathy for them, but often remarks that she feels sorry for them. 'You and me, we understand,' is one of her favourite conclusions, and it is always easier to agree with her. Every time she comes into my room I wonder which of my principles will be sacrificed or subjugated for the duration of her stay. In nine years very little has changed. I still think of them as principles but in reality they amount to little more than my own instinctive prejudices.

'Mr Farouk,' she continued, 'has his ways.'

'I don't doubt it.'

'You know something?'

'No more than anyone else. He thinks people are following him.'

'Following him,' she added derisively. 'Who'd want to follow him?'

'He thinks someone is spying on him.' A half lie.

'And you believe him?'

I shook my head.

'No, of course you don't. Nobody in their right mind would believe him.'

I nodded. A hundred fine distinctions were drawn between us every day. Every one of us created spaces and connections when it suited, and it was only when something happened to upset the fine balance of our relationships that we felt uneasy. Except Farouk, who felt constantly uneasy and who, in all likelihood, probably had very good reason to feel uneasy. If anyone *was* following him then it would very likely turn out to be the father of an Arab youth or a plainclothes policeman. The thought made me smile, and seeing me smile made Mrs D smile.

'I have to be very careful, you understand, on who I take in.' She made living with her sound like a privilege.

'You can't be too careful,' I said.

'That's right. That's perfectly right.'

It was worth a second cigarette. When that was finished I told her I had to go out. She said it had started to rain. I said I had a coat. She said she'd seen it and that it was too thin. I asked her the time and then behaved as though I was late for an appointment.

I left the house and walked in a wide circle for an hour. When I returned I held my coat in front of the fire and watched the steam rise from it. I heard her downstairs, singing, and laying a table with crockery and glasses. There were times when it became an almost physical necessity to get out of the house.

He introduced himself as Farouk. We called him Farouk and he laughed, shook his head and corrected us. It was part of a longer name. He repeated it in full, insisting that it was how he should be addressed. He said it as though it were his last proud possession. We tried and failed, and from then on he was known simply as Farouk. He insisted it was too formal, but it was the best we were prepared to do.

I am beginning to suffer from insomnia, lying awake until four, sometimes five in the morning, and listening to the noises of the house below and above me. Others are awake. Footsteps three floors up reverberate and pulled plugs click from their sockets.

A month after my arrival I fell ill. A doctor arranged for me to have an X-ray taken of my stomach and a week later informed me that I had an ulcer and gave me a prescription. I became suddenly seriously ill and demanded to know more. His waiting room was filled with other patients waiting to know. I walked through them, silently demanding that they should feel sorry for me. I resented a crying child because it diverted attention from my own suffering. I left the building trying to imagine what the growth inside me would look like if I could see it.

After a month of relative abstinence and treatment I was declared cured. I felt cheated. Mrs D continued to bring me milk and I regretted having told her. She discussed her own body and lifted her blouse an inch to show me a scar on what had once been her waist. It was the same white skin I saw in the dream. When I was pronounced cured she arrived one evening with a bottle of gin and said that the doctors didn't know what they were talking about. After drinking some I felt sick. I told her and she behaved as though I'd accepted with the sole purpose of proving them right and her wrong. Afterwards I saw nothing of her for almost a fortnight. It was my first real memory of my time in the house.

Lynette was her real name. Lynette Mary Elizabeth. Mary after her mother, Elizabeth after her grandmother, both after royalty. It was that kind of family – no real idea of tradition, just a sort of thoughtless perpetuation. The men had long since become weak and forgettable and had a tendency to die well before their wives. This suited the women, who thrived. Some even remarried and thus extended what little pleasure there was to be gained from outliving more than one husband. I mention all this because twelve years ago I married Lynette. We had four bad years together.

The name embarrassed me, she embarrassed me, I stopped having even the slightest feeling for her and she still embarrassed me. I fought with her, I left her, I came to live here and even now the memory of her can still embarrass me. The problem began the day after we were married – the day I sat back and watched her turn into her mother.

In truth, it began long before then, but to admit to that would require too great a confession. In the past nine years I have deceived myself into believing a great deal I would not previously have thought possible.

Before we were married I tried calling her Lynn and she always corrected me. After we were married I stopped trying.

I confessed my ambition to her. She took it well, said it was nice, that everyone should have at least one ambition. She had hers. Before we were married that was how everything was: things were nice, things were not nice. I married her confident in the belief that I would be successful at what I wanted to do. It is why I am now what I am. One thing led directly to another. I lost a succession of jobs, always looking ahead to the days when I would be looking back. I can remember ten-year-old conversations to the word. None of it ever leaves me. That too is why I am what I am, and why, ultimately, I left her and she let me go.

When I went out she often used to pick up one of her small dogs and hold it to the window, waving its paw at me as I walked down the garden path and out into the road.

Before, when people asked, 'How's Lynette?' I would always reply, 'Oh, Lynn. You mean Lynn.'

She used to pick up the dogs and speak to them, manipulating their paws as though they were puppets. Low voices for the dogs, high for the bitches. They had eyes like brown marbles, glassy and pathetic, as though they were about to weep. When they were ill or cold their eyes watered and she cossetted them as though they were crying children.

She used to say things like 'Give Mummy a kiss', and force their muzzles into her face. She kissed their heads and cheeks, and when I said it was unhygienic she simply stared at me disbelievingly. It all added up.

I have a paraffin heater which, on the few occasions I use it, fills my room with fumes and condensation. Mrs D expects daily to find me dead. I do my best to reassure her. It is never enough. The heater is unreliable, a death trap, there are reports in the papers almost daily . . . There is a rule about storing paraffin in the rooms, an insurance clause. I will cause an explosion and we will all be burned alive, horribly, agonizingly, in our beds. All this she has repeated to anyone who will listen. I point out to her that there are similar heaters in some of the other rooms. We will all be blown up and burned alive ten times over. I am being selfish, thinking only of myself – *I* have access to the fire escape. She gains the support of the Patels by telling them that they, on the other hand, do not. In addition to which they also have two small children. I am being told all this for my own good. I am expected to be grateful.

Four streets away a launderette and line of familiar shops have been demolished. The situation requires reassessment. No matter how calmly Mrs D might attempt to respond to the events beyond the house, panic seems always to be the most convenient answer. Local newspapers report our plight. She begins to refer to what is happening to us as Our Plight. Less than a mile away an underground train has been derailed, killing two passengers. Everyone in the city seems to be suffering.

A new tenant has moved into one of the third-floor rooms. He is a body-builder, building for himself the perfect body. His progress to date is only too evident, even through the heavy coats and scarves that he wears. His neck is thick and tapers outwards from his chin. When he speaks his facial muscles flex and relax, emphasizing and then detracting from whatever he has to say, which is usually very little, except how he is progressing and how unfit and undernourished the rest of us are.

On the day of his arrival he wore only a T-shirt and shorts, revealing his back and perfect stomach. Two similarly constructed friends helped carry his belongings up the stairs. Every load, it seemed, contained a full-length mirror. I have been inside his room. The mirrors line two walls and around them are scattered the contraptions with which he is building his body. With the exception of Farouk, we all resent his presence. I think of him as 'Atlas'. The West Indians ignore him because he offended them on the day of his arrival, and Mr Patel and his wife side with me. Farouk spends a lot of time examining the posters of muscle-bound men which adorn the mirror-free walls. I am not sure what Mrs D thinks. She was out when the mirrors and weights were brought in and she seldom ventures as high as the third floor.

I have not yet been invited to feel a clenched muscle, but it is what I expect every time I see him. He stands in poses, bending his legs and gripping his forearms, and making small, involuntary grunts at some hidden internal effort. I tell him I am impressed and he tells me I should do something about my own body. He touches my arm and pulls a face of disgust.

The men who helped him move in return frequently. Occasionally it is possible to hear them sighing and grunting in unison.

Mr Patel once remarked to Atlas that he must be very proud of his body and Atlas replied that everyone had a responsibility to look after themselves. Mr Patel said he was right. Atlas rattled a bottle of pills and listed for us what they did for him. Mr Patel was impressed. He lifted the lid of the saucepan he held on the cooker, the contents of which seldom varied, each meal having its foundations in whatever remained from the day before.

Atlas has painted the door to his room scarlet and to it he has fixed a plaque announcing his presence. None of the other rooms draw attention to their occupants. I pointed this out to Mrs D. She said she thought it would brighten the place up, and I knew exactly where I stood.

Directly above me there lives a Negro and his girl. It is how I think of and refer to them. They are both unemployed and spend most of their days together in the room. If they have names I am not alone in not knowing them. Their footsteps across the floor above me are the softest in the house. They laugh a lot and play the same few records over and over. Mrs D regrets having let the room to them. The man moves through the house with an air of supreme indifference. He listens to what we have to say to him and if he chooses to answer he does so. Otherwise he ignores us. The girl seems more friendly, but subdued in his presence. She walks behind him and takes her cues from him. She sings along with the records and has a good voice.

I rent a single room with access to a shared bathroom and a cramped kitchen partitioned from a wide landing on the first floor. There are missing tiles in the bathroom, and beneath them black mould. The tap drips continuously and neither I nor any of the others use the bath. The kitchen consists of a sink, a cupboard and a small cooker. Its chief purpose seems to be to ensure that we look elsewhere for our meals. Whenever one of us uses the cooker the smell of the meal fills the house for a day. Whenever the Patels use it, the smell persists for a week.

When I told Mrs D what I was she insisted that I took the room with two windows, 'for the light'. I told her she was confusing me with an artist and she accused me of being modest. Most of our exchanges began and ended at such tangents.

The room sets me apart. When she discusses the other tenants with me she raises her eyes and lowers her voice. We are 'us', they are 'them'. I try to convince myself that we are all in the same situation and that they too have no real existence elsewhere. Their various arrivals and departures are frequent and, by virtue of my nine years, I have become, apart from Mrs D, the house's only semi-permanent resident. This is an achievement of sorts. This also sets me apart.

There was no element of choice involved when I took the room. I walked away from Lynette, rode for an hour on a bus, stopped at the first newsagent's window I came to, read a card and arrived. Mrs D inspected me in the daylight and then again in the light of her hallway. She looked at the few belongings I had with me and said she wasn't certain. She asked me what I did. I told her. She called me a 'Professional Gentleman' and offered me the room. It suited her to say it and me to hear it. She searched a chest-of-drawers for the key. I waited in the hallway, looking up at the brown faces looking down at me. As we climbed the stairs they withdrew. It made my arrival something of an occasion. I stayed.

I spent the whole of my first night drinking supermarket whisky and sitting by the window, listening to the other tenants as they arrived home and went out again.

Mrs D entered the room ahead of me, took a deep breath and pulled a face. I told her the room was precisely what I wanted. She did her best. She outlined her terms and said they were reasonable. I paid her and she moved around the room ahead of me, making a mental inventory of its few shabby contents.

'Fully furnished,' I said, referring to the card in the window. She pointed to the pictures on the wall and rattled the cutlery in the drawer of the sink unit, beneath which lay a pool of water. She turned on both taps and told me how to get hot water. I would be there a month at the most. I treated it all as a joke.

The smell from the landing filled the room. She had had a dream of a respectable boarding house full of Professional Gentlemen and had come to this. She would have preferred somewhere near the sea. She had been born in a house less than half a mile from this one and her mother had died at a point along a line between the two. She tested the two light fittings, moving the bulb from one to the other. She seemed pleased and surprised that they both worked. We listened together to the subterranean rumbles of the underground.

One wall was papered in gold and crimson. She ran a palm over its embossed surface and told me to do the same. An impressive fireplace had been boarded over, flecks of marble still showing through the chipped paint.

There were two pictures in the room – one of a ginger kitten playing with a ball of wool. 'Genuine fur.' She stroked it. The other was of Dedham Mill, the underlying painting recreated in the brushstrokes of its heavily applied varnish. I did everything she told me to and agreed with everything she said. I was still above it all, looking down and making decisions about what happened next.

In the hallway Little Lord Fauntleroy sat beneath a tree in his velvet suit and cried. She said she liked to have paintings around her. In winter it was possible to pass only a foot from the crying boy and not realize he existed.

That was nine years ago. Very little about the room has changed. It depressed me then, it depresses me now. It might be any one of ten thousand others within hearing distance of the trains.

With her increasing success at the dog shows, Lynette began to spend longer periods away from home, often two or three weekends a month at the height of the season. She graduated from local to national shows and by her fourth year of showing there was so much silver plate in the house that she had burglar alarms fitted. On the days when the bright afternoon sunlight shone in, it sometimes seemed as though the room in which the trophies were kept was on fire. I knew she was striving for greater things when the certificates began to be left unframed, simply collected in a drawer to show to prospective buyers.

In her third year she won a local Small Businessman's award for the most imaginative enterprise in her region. She looked upon it as having 'arrived'. She was presented with the award at a dinner dance. Dinner dances were her favourite form of entertainment and she insisted that I attend with her, buying me a new suit for the occasion. Afterwards she pointed out the words 'Most Imaginative' on the certificate and made a smug, unspoken comparison between what she did and what I did. By then she employed two helpers, had doubled the size of the kennels and earned enough to be able to pay her mother on the days she came to help. Her mother was the first of her employees to wear the ridiculous kennel-maid's outfit, for which Lynette had also paid. The others had no choice but to follow suit.

I had disliked her mother ever since our first eventful meeting. I wasn't what she'd hoped for; her daughter could do much better. She made all this clear to me in as many ways as possible without actually saying it. I rose to the challenge. The better I got to know her, the more I found to dislike about her. I watched her when I should have been watching Lynette, and vice versa. They were the same woman all along.

Lynette and I passed temporarily through a better patch. I remained at home each weekend during Lynette's absence, feeding and cleaning out the dogs and guarding the house. She rang each morning and evening, and after each show she called with her news of success or failure. She spoke breathlessly, as though I'd been waiting anxiously for the news. I was the first to hear it, an honour. It bored me. I told her so. I resented the dogs their easy successes, but I kept that to myself. Hearing the excitement in her voice I knew precisely how far apart we had grown.

On Saturdays a schoolgirl arrived to help with the grooming and trimming of the dogs. In Lynette's absence I sat with the three assistants during their lunch break. They spoke about the dogs in the same disinterested tone with which they spoke about everything else. Initially, my presence made them feel uncomfortable. They behaved as though they had been told something about me which they had been sworn not to reveal. The schoolgirl began to flirt with me, brushing invisible dog hairs from her shoulders and breasts. She insisted that I put ointment on her chin where one of the dogs had caught her with its paw. After that I tried to avoid her. I heard the three of them laughing, their voices amplified by the kennels. When I appeared they stopped, exchanged glances and dispersed. In the house I sat in the bedroom and tried to write. Nothing happened. I began to make excuses.

Whenever I was at home alone Lynette's mother stayed away. She arrived once having confused her dates. Finding me alone, she accused me of making her daughter's life a misery. I asked her if she'd had a good look at her daughter recently. She asked me what I meant. When I explained she sat speechless, holding her hand over her heart as though it might explode at any second and leave me having to live with being responsible for her death for the rest of my life. I took a perverse pleasure in my cruelty, knowing that nothing she would repeat to Lynette wouldn't already have been said before. She spluttered, small bubbles forming on her lips. I described her daughter and what had happened to us in the minutest detail. But she preferred to look at the trophies and certificates, pointing to these as the true indicators of what was happening. She accused me of being an Evil Man, Genuinely Evil. She had made allowances, she said, but never again.

When Lynette rang I told her what had happened. But the dog of the day hadn't been placed and so I doubt if anything I said even registered.

A week after my arrival Mrs D began telling me the stories of her two husbands. She listed their qualities and faults on the fingers of each hand, raising and lowering her palms until a balance was achieved. The second had been no better than the first, and the first no better than any of the other men from whom she might have chosen. She spoke and sighed like a woman who had once possessed a great beauty, but who had squandered it.

We sat in her room. It was better furnished and decorated than all the others, but in its essentials was no different. Like my own, one end had a view over the garden, the other out on to the street. We drank tea and she showed me photographs.

'A triumph of hope over experience,' I said.

'What?'

'A second marriage.'

'Oh.' She smiled and watched me suspiciously, as though I had deliberately exhibited my cleverness at her expense.

'Oscar Wilde,' I said.

'Oh,' she said, and drank her tea as she considered how to change the subject. I soon realized that the discussion of her husbands and her marriages was her prerogative alone. I wondered if either of the men had died and disappointed her expectations. It was how she would have referred to it.

'A writer like yourself, was he?' She stared directly at me.

I nodded, defeated. 'He was.'

'Dead?'

'Yes.'

'Shame.'

'Yes.'

'Still . . .' She said 'Shame' again.

Since my arrival I had done nothing. I was still above it all, but sinking. I suppose I was still half hoping for the arrival of a contrite Lynette.

Mrs D asked me if I was married. I confessed that I was.

'And . . .?'

'We . . .'

She was shaking her head before I'd started. A short silence followed. She returned to her husbands, speaking as though each bad memory and experience had remained with her to the exclusion of all else. As she spoke, she rubbed her arms and asked me if I understood. I said I did. She said she appreciated having someone civilized to talk to and I wondered how many times she'd been through the same lengthy, self-indulgent routine. She referred to herself as having gone from being an attractive woman to an attractive proposition, saying it as though she might have possessed a hidden wealth. But I knew that what she meant was the house above us.

Even then, nine years ago, she was anxious at the proposal to demolish the house and surrounding streets. At the time I considered the idea a good one. Five years later it began, and now, three years after the first houses were flattened, those on either side of us are being prepared. She has shown me an old letter promising that no homes would be demolished until every householder had been satisfactorily rehoused. Few of the tenants in the houses already torn down complained about their rights. Most simply moved outwards to the nearest vacancies and began again.

Yesterday I watched a perfect formation of geese pass above the city, moving as though they were a single creature, silently and effortlessly, out of place above a horizon unbroken by the outline of a single tree. I waited to see if others might follow. None appeared.

The process of demolition and renewal continues around us. Demolition mostly, but with the promise of re-growth in the maps and plans displayed in the foyer of the Town Hall.

Mrs D continues to regard what is happening as a kind of conspiracy against her, and lives in a state of permanent crisis. There are days when meeting her is almost painful. She insists that we all agree with her, and because of what she is and what we are, we do.

On the mantelpiece of her room she has displayed a half pane of glass with its jagged edge rising to a peak between her husbands. She insists that we examine it. She says she found it on her doorstep and that it was put there to intimidate her. She says she knows where the glass has come from. She even knows who put it there. Every time she says it she causes whoever is listening to feel guilty, as though they themselves had something to gain by her misery and removal.

There are a thousand broken windows from which the glass might have come and so we take neither her claims nor threats seriously.

I watched her yesterday with Atlas. He stood beside her and looked concerned as she told him of the plot against us. We are all included. When she asked if he wanted to see the glass he said he did. I suspected his motives, I suspected hers. Normally she would have insisted rather than asked. They were together in her room for almost an hour. They came out once and stood briefly in the doorway. She pointed out to him the broken window from which she believed the glass to have come. In the fanlight above them were a dozen panels of coloured glass arranged in a symmetrical pattern.

One of the panels was cracked and another had been replaced by a small square of ordinary glass. I have often wondered who would have so little imagination as to replace the few inches of colour with such ordinariness. It was almost as though the house itself had at some time responded to its own inevitable decline. The light from the hallway shone through the door, casting the shadows of Atlas and Mrs D ahead of them and speckling their backs with flecks of blue, red and green. I listened to their conversation, reassured by its familiarity.

Farouk arrived and forced them both into silence. They watched him climb the stairs. When he greeted them they turned away, refusing to speak, even to each other, in his presence. I watched them through a gap in my door. When Farouk had gone Mrs D whispered something and Atlas laughed. She asked him to carry the glass back to her mantelpiece. She refused now to touch it.

Above me I heard Farouk singing one of his rising and falling, warbling and quavering Arab songs. The Negro and his girl had their door open and a record playing. We have all mastered the art of announcing ourselves, at being at once unseen and taken into consideration. The staircase was cold from the front door having been open for so long.

Perhaps Mrs D thinks we will support her in her useless campaign. Perhaps she has taken it for granted all along. She is far from ignorant of our vulnerability and perhaps her own sudden exposure has made her believe a new bond has been forged between us. She is wrong. She is the captain and we are the ship's rats. When we reach the point of no return she will no more think of doing anything for us than we would of asking her to.

Initially, the terraces of houses were demolished completely and left as neat, room-high mounds of brick and moulding, with paths between them. Where the doors had been flanked by decorative stone pillars, these were left standing. They rose above the rubble and gave its sprawling mounds the appearance of ancient ruins, of a great civilization surviving in only its strongest features.

Where the houses are still not completely flattened they are left as gutted shells with precarious staircases and hanging floors. Fires are started inside them. The demolition workers move through the rising dust and debris as though nothing were happening. We watch them but they pay us no attention.

At nights and weekends the shells are occupied by vagrants who light their own fires. Occasionally they congregate in the late afternoon, waiting for the sites to clear. Some of the workers throw bricks at them as though they were dogs come to scavenge. The vagrants gather in groups, standing without speaking to each other. Their faces are hard to see, but they are easily distinguishable. The same figures return each day. They move into the empty houses together and once inside they disappear. I have seldom seen any of them come out into the street in the morning, and they are careful not to let the demolition workers catch them. They leave behind them their own detritus, but this is quickly absorbed into the sediment of the houses.

At weekends, when the sites are empty, I cross the street to inspect the week's progress. I disturb the new inhabitants and hear them moving from room to room, seeking to avoid rather than confront me. The piles of rubble and parts of unsafe floors collapse behind them. The sound of smashing glass is something to which we have all become accustomed, Mrs D especially. She refers to the vagrants as animals, using the word at every opportunity. They are barely human. They are no better than animals. They are not even animals. It varies. She will be saying it now to Atlas. And he will be agreeing with her. I have seen the vagrants throw stones at stray dogs and at the few children who venture on to the site. Spotlights were mounted but were quickly broken. A high mesh fence was erected, but this too was swiftly breached.

Mrs D will take the piece of glass into a court of law and produce it as evidence of intimidation and victimization. Atlas will be called as her witness and he will repeat everything she has told him to say. Then she will be handsomely compensated and they will move away together to live in the country. She talks a lot about compensation, asking us if we know where it comes from, who pays it and how to claim it. I have told her repeatedly that the forms she has received will contain all the necessary information. But she refuses to open them, and even by suggesting that she should, I am considered to have joined the conspiracy against her. She believes that simply by reading the contents of the envelopes she will in some way have acquiesced to their demands and contributed towards her own downfall.

Beneath me the door opens and I stand at my own to overhear what is said. She is helping Atlas on with his coat for the short, cold journey up to his room. There is music behind them and an illusory flush of warmth from the overhead light. She speaks to him, but their voices are low and I cannot hear.

They are interrupted a second time by the arrival of the West Indians, who stand in the hallway shaking the rain from their jackets and slapping the wall in their search for the switch. I know to the inch where to find it, but they never do. They move from the hallway on to the stairs. Atlas and Mrs D stand silently in the shadow of the passage leading to her room.

It is six o'clock, and the hours between now and nine often seem to be the longest of the day.

Atlas appears on the stairs, coming up them three at a time, stopping when he sees me and breathing deeply. He is tanned and we are all pale. He nods at the cigarette in my hand and tuts. It is a form of greeting. I say that we are all killing ourselves one way or another.

'Not me,' he says. 'Not me.'

I ask him if he happens to have seen Mrs D. He glances at me suspiciously and continues up to his room without answering, still three steps at a time, four strides up each flight.

At the first stroke the skin parted from the tip of her breast to her navel. The distance was short, a matter of a few inches. It peeled open into a perfect bloody eclipse. We studied it and were satisfied with the result. The body settled itself more comfortably on to the worn carpet. It asked for something to eat and the room became saturated with the smell of cooking. The others became impatient and I went on. Atlas stood on one leg, raising and lowering the other, clasping it around the knee.

I made the second cut at right angles to the first, then a third and fourth at diagonals, until the petals of a simple flower opened against the skin. I was showing off, turning a necessity into an art. Even the body leaned forward to see. But as it did so the effect was ruined and the blood which had so far been contained beneath the skin was smeared and the perfect shape was lost. The illusion of power is beginning to fade, and the dream itself is failing, becoming less predictable and precise.

Everything I used to do to fill my days has now become too much of an effort. I allow myself to be too easily distracted. I search out distractions in the minutiae of the routine of the house. I write a sentence and spend an hour searching out its imperfections. At the end of the day I screw up the paper and throw it carefully down. I prove to myself that I am still a writer. It is the weakest of my deceptions. The balls of paper remain in place for a week. They are the chips beneath the bench on which a block of marble is being chiselled to nothing in the hope and expectation that the statue within will reveal itself, requiring simply to be exposed. Still the writer.

Mrs D remarks on the balls of paper and says she understands. One day I will ask her precisely *what* she understands. On my table there are sheets half filled with writing which have remained untouched for months. In the absence of anything new I spread these out to maintain appearances and momentum. It is a slow, self-defeating existence, but it provides me with no challenge greater than that which I am able to meet or can afford to ignore. I will rise like a phoenix from the ruins of the house. I am awaiting a revival.

Mr Patel talks to me about the great books of India, of which he knows very little. He makes patterns in the air with the wooden spoon with which he is stirring his saucepan of oily vegetables. Occasionally the door to his room opens and his wife appears. When she sees me she looks annoyed and gestures to him to hurry. He tests the pan, points to me, taps his forehead and shrugs. I mime my greetings to her.

'Ah, women,' he sighs, and looks instantly dejected, as though everything in his life has disappointed him.

'Ah, yes, women, wives,' I add.

'Mrs D,' he says, pulling another face.

From inside his room the sound of his wife's shouting rises to a crescendo and then subsides. Their two small children begin to cry.

'Ah, children,' he says, and turns back to his saucepan.

Later I recorded the conversation exactly as it had taken place. We spoke of the approaching winter and of the difficulty of keeping the rooms warm. He considered everything I said, answered and sighed. Mrs D shouted up the stairs and he removed his pan from the cooker and ran with it to his room.

Occasionally, late at night, and purely for effect, I arrange my anglepoise lamp above my typewriter, insert a sheet of old typing and stand an empty glass beside it. Then I study the composition from the far side of the room. If someone were to knock and enter and see the arrangement, the illusion would be complete. Then I sit and tap out lines of gibberish in black and red.

I hear people coming and going on the landing outside. Occasionally there are pauses, as though someone were about to knock. In the seconds before the knock – which seldom materializes – the noises of the entire house become amplified: the Patel children crying, their mother shouting; the West Indians laughing and exaggerating their greetings, their every silence filled with music; Mrs D singing to the radio; the opening and closing of doors, televisions; the scrape of furniture and running water. They all precede the silent knock, and then follow it away.

Even on the brightest of days there is a shadow at the centre of my room where the sunlight does not reach. I sit in the middle of it and it seems to me to be the precise point at which I have arrived, and at which I should remain. I still cannot help thinking of Lynette every time a dog barks in the street, or whenever they appear on television commercials pawing tins of unopened food. Last month I watched Crufts, expecting at any moment to hear her name and to see her face filling the screen, kissing the head of one of the dogs which had made her so suddenly famous.

The distinctions between what I believe to be the truth and what I know to be part of the illusion are no longer as well defined as they used to be. The thought is a comforting one, but only for as long as I continue to understand and cling to my reasons for establishing it.

I visited the zoo with Farouk. Half-price entrance, a publicity stunt. He invited me and insisted on paying. On the journey there he told me of the job he had recently got at a night-club in the city. Every time he mentioned the name he checked his collar and straightened his tie. There was a uniform with the job, an evening jacket. The collar of his shirt was too large and hung over his jacket.

He presented himself for my inspection at nine in the morning and I complimented him on his appearance. He said it was nothing and proceeded to tell me how much he had paid for almost everything he was wearing. I asked him about his new job and he went into another routine of telling me how much responsibility it entailed and how highly regarded he was by the club owner. I asked him what sort of club it was and he said I wouldn't be interested. He told me instead about his shoes. He leaves the house at nine each evening and returns at ten or eleven the following morning. He refers to the job as his 'Great Fortune'.

He smelt strongly of after-shave and people passing us on the bus sniffed the air. Several greeted him and paused briefly to talk. He introduced me to them. Some looked at me puzzled and then offered to shake my hand, which was difficult in the confined space. I began to wonder if I hadn't misinterpreted his offer. He caught one of my worried looks and made an effort to put me at ease. He told me he valued my friendship. It was probably the wrong thing for him to say, but I told him I understood.

We changed buses and walked the remaining distance to the zoo. He stood looking up at the entrance and said he wished we had a camera. I told him there would be postcards on sale inside. We went in. I was about to suggest a route which would include most of what there was to be seen, when he insisted that we visit the cafeteria. I followed him in. He lit a cigarette, sipped at his coffee and announced that coming to the zoo had been a lifelong ambition. He began to list the animals he wanted to see and I promised him we would see them all. The walls of the cafeteria were covered with posters depicting brilliantly coloured tropical birds, against which even he looked drab and uninteresting. He asked if I knew their names.

He wanted first to see the big cats. We followed the signs. The lions disappointed him, disappointed us both. Ocasionally one of them rose, walked a few paces and flopped down again. Farouk slapped his palms against the railing separating them from us. He spoke to them in his own language and then threw up his hands in despair. The situation was saved by the sight of a weary male's attempts to mount an equally weary female. Farouk moved along the wall for a better view. He shouted words of encouragement and, when the lion finally succeeded in several seconds' penetration, he applauded. Other visitors moved quickly past us.

In the next cage the tigers were conspicuous by their absence and the remaining cats were disappointingly small and tame. A keeper stroked the belly of a lynx, posing beside the animal for photographs. Farouk pretended he had a camera, pointed his hands and said 'Click'.

In the Reptile House he tapped on the glass to the snakes and lizards and they hid from us under stones. Outside he laughed at a miserable looking pack of hyenas as they scavenged for food along the edge of their compound.

Overall the visit disappointed and saddened him. Over lunch he made plans to visit the Planetarium and Buckingham Palace. I asked him if he'd never seen the latter. He said something about the Queen and smiled. We sat in another cafeteria and ate sandwiches. He seemed reluctant to go back out and complete our tour. I asked him if there were zoos in his country, still not entirely certain where that was.

'No, only animals.'

He took out his wallet and showed me photographs of his mother and assorted aunts, uncles, brothers and sisters. He said he would buy postcards of the animals and send them home. When I asked him if he missed his family he shook his head and changed the subject.

When we eventually left the cafeteria he complained that his legs ached from standing so long.

At the souvenir shop he bought a car sticker announcing that he had been to the zoo. I collected some postcards together for him, placing one of a roaring lion on top. He asked if I were thinking of buying any. When I said I wasn't he left me to inspect the shelves of small plastic animals. His spirits rose when he saw the display of slides. He picked out several and said that these were what he wanted. These were what he would send home. I said that I thought his decision unwise and told him how the slides had been taken and what equipment would be needed to view them properly. But my explanation made him even more determined to buy them. I realized only afterwards what the arrival of these slides would suggest and how much he would achieve by sending them. I congratulated him on his choice.

On our return journey he inspected the slides against the lights of the bus. He said he would begin a collection of all the famous landmarks. I told him it would be cheaper for him to buy a camera and take his own. The idea appealed to him and he suggested that I should accompany him. I said I knew nothing about cameras, but he only laughed and patted my back.

The sticker of the zoo appeared on his door the next morning, and was added to over the following weeks by many more. I was surprised at the determination with which he put his plan into action and at the extent of his travels round the city. I also wondered at the size of his photographic collection and what his distant family thought of it all.

Then he began to return with stickers bearing more gimmicky designs, and some with lewd jokes and motifs. Mrs D said she couldn't bring herself to complain at the appearance of his door because he seemed so excited, and because on several occasions he had returned with duplicate stickers and presented them to her as gifts. He also began to borrow library books, and afterwards to speak with some authority on dates and places, dimensions and events, kings and queens. He memorized small speeches by heart.

A month after our visit to the zoo I saw him emerge from a gift shop carrying a collection of stickers. He stood in the street and examined them. I turned away from him to avoid being seen.

As winter drew on he explained that he was going on fewer outings because he had been given more responsibilities by his employer. The stickers stopped appearing on his door, and those that were already there began to peel and come loose.

His surreptitious trips up and down the fire escape resumed. On one occasion I looked out and saw the face of a youth only inches from my window, his startled eyes like those of a deer caught in the headlights of a car. Farouk appeared beside him, pushed the boy away and smiled in at me, his finger over his lips. I nodded to him and he disappeared up into the darkness.

The rain has begun to drip into my room above the front bay window. Its motion and the noise it makes have become an obsession. On the few occasions I am able to clear my mind it is filled with the noise of the rain. I have positioned a saucepan under the drip, and into it I have put a cloth to deaden the noise. It has been raining almost continuously for three days and coming into my room for the past two. There is a rose-shaped stain on the ceiling through which a pattern of laths is becoming increasingly visible. There is no hole as such, just a point at which the seeping water collects and from which it drips. Occasionally it falls from elsewhere within the patch and misses the pan completely. I have tried unsuccessfully to trace the source of the leak. The nearest I can get is the lead flashing above the window, some of which must be loose, allowing the strong wind to force the water between it and the brick wall.

Since the water started coming in my mind has been concentrated. I have devised a dozen solutions to the problem. Mrs D will probably sympathize and berate the local builder who arrived ten years ago to fix the same leak. Just before my time. But she won't really care, and it is unlikely that she will do anything about it.

Last night a second damp patch appeared, this time around the light fitting at the same end of the room. The water travelled down the flex and dripped from the bulb. I removed this, but was unable to turn off the power. I caught this second leak in an empty tin, which I emptied at intervals into the saucepan. By morning the tin had overflowed and the carpet around it was saturated. I had woken in the night and had listened to the two drips, timing them against each other and noting the differences in their pitch. After a particularly strong gust of wind, the leak from above the light came in as a brief but continuous stream for several seconds, hanging against the street lights like a thread from floor to ceiling. I watched it but was too tired and cold to attempt to remedy it.

I mentioned the leaks twice to Mrs D, and the second time she looked offended and asked me if I was *still* complaining.

Mrs D read an account in the newspaper of a man south of the river who had earned himself a place in the record books by reading and then eating the complete works of Shakespeare in a single week.

'He actually *read* them?' I said.

She said she wasn't surprised: it was an uncivilized place, south of the river. It was what her grandmother had told her mother, and what her mother had told her. The man was in the record books under the heading Literary Feats.

She said her mother had been a great one for Shakespeare.

'All's Well that Ends Well,' I said.

'Ah,' she sighed.

She said she'd read somewhere that a row of monkeys sitting at typewriters had produced every one of Shakespeare's plays entirely by chance. She began to list the ones she thought her mother had seen, or read, or heard of: '*Midsummer Night's Dream, Romeo and Juliet, Pride and Prejudice, King Lear.*' She sighed again after each name.

I said I thought it a shame to have eaten them all at a single sitting.

She said she supposed I was right, and looked at me in a way that suggested she thought I too might be capable of such a feat. Being a writer, that was.

'I could nibble on Céline or Genet,' I suggested. She said they sounded like French perfumes.

I asked her if she knew that the story of Frankenstein had been conceived by a teenage girl. She asked me if I was sure. When I convinced her that I was, she said you could never tell what people were thinking simply by looking at them. She asked me if the girl had lived south of the river and I said she had. This pleased her and she said it was where that kind of writer belonged.

Plans for the breeding kennels were in hand well before the wedding. They were Lynette's 'Dream Come True', and I had originally intended having no part in the running of them. From breeding she progressed to showing, selling the unsuccessful animals to almost every other member of her family.

The number of dogs fluctuated, but settled eventually at around three dozen: a dozen each of miniature poodles and Yorkshire terriers and a further dozen assorted, including chihuahuas and pekinese, all equally small and trembly.

After each sale Lynette recorded the details in her breeding book and almost cried. She kissed the dogs as she handed them over and instructed them to be good. Included in their price was a certificate and flimsy red bow tied between their ears. Signing out the bitches for breeding was even worse. Then she behaved like a Victorian mother on the eve of her daughter's wedding. The animal in question was usually brought into the house the night before and cossetted on her knee in front of the fire. When I suggested to her that the dogs might actually enjoy what they were getting she got in a rage and then ignored me.

Each dog was provided with an individual raised bedding area which opened out on to a long narrow run, separated from its neighbours by high mesh fencing. The kennels began at the bottom of the garden and were screened from the houses on either side by red and yellow, artificial-looking conifers. Every six months they were inspected by an environmental health officer. Lynette also made a point of inviting the RSPCA. They both came, inspected, listened to the tales of her sales and showing successes and commended her for keeping the cleanest kennels in the district. I wanted to ask them how many others there were.

Beyond the kennels was an area of open land used as rough pasture for a number of worn and useless horses, and as a dump for fridges, prams, washing machines and the occasional car. Gangs of youths roamed the land, frightening the horses and chasing them as they galloped away. They disturbed the dogs and set off chain reactions of howling and whining late at night.

I once suggested to Lynette that she should build up a circus act or train the dogs for television work. She accused me of being mercenary. I stood my ground and she ignored me for a week. She became the family success and everyone tried to become involved. Even her refusal to have children was eventually accepted by a family whose sole aim often appeared to be little more than its own prolific regeneration. That anyone should actually consider themselves in a position to decide *not* to have children was the greatest shock to be overcome. But it was, and during the last year or so the unspoken blame was shifted from her to me.

I once dreamt of her in a circus tent and of the small dogs bouncing through flaming hoops, each one catching fire as it passed through and then forming into a living pyrotechnic display completed by Lynette herself as an outline of waving flames. The dogs would finish as balls of charred meat, but she would rise again and continue.

Above me, the music began mid-morning and continued until the early hours of the following day. I went down to Mrs D to complain. She wanted me to stay and talk to her. I told her I was working and she seemed even more reluctant to do anything about the noise. Eventually she followed me up the stairs.

Already gathered outside the offending room were Mrs Patel and her two children, and the West Indians from the attic. Mrs Patel stood with her hands over her ears and instructed her children to do the same. The West Indians slapped their hands together and said they wanted to join the party. Mrs D informed them that there were no parties in her house. 'No, ma'am.' 'No, sir.' They pulled servile faces and then laughed at her behind her back. She knocked on the door. Nothing. She knocked again and then instructed me to do the same. I knocked with her and Mrs Patel shouted.

The door was opened by the tall Negro. He had a twisted mane of hair over his shoulders and was naked to the waist. He seemed only half awake.

'What you want?' The music swept out of the room behind him and hit us like a warm wind.

I pointed to Mrs D but she seemed uncertain. To encourage her, Mrs Patel shouted something in Hindi, or whatever. I suddenly realized how irritating and insignificant we must all have seemed to the half-awake man.

His girlfriend appeared behind him. She was dressed only in a sheet, which she held between her forefinger and thumb above her breasts.

Mrs D whispered to me that she had taken them as man and wife. I knew that even *she* could not have believed that. The thought also occurred that she might have told the others that she had taken me as a writer.

The man and girl stood like an African warrior king and his queen. The girl held a cigarette, placing it between her lips for only the briefest of sucks. The two West Indians pushed forward and waved at her. Mrs Patel gave Mrs D a push in the small of her back. Mrs D resented this and told her so. Mrs Patel understood nothing and simply nodded.

'What we want . . .' Mrs D began, looking around at us all, 'What we want is for you to stop that racket.' She pronounced each word carefully. There could be no doubt as to what we wanted. The girl turned down the volume and returned to the door. They had defeated us by the simplicity of their solution.

'Now what you want?' the girl asked. She released her grip on the sheet and I watched her, expecting it to fall away and reveal the most perfect body I had ever seen.

'Too loud,' Mrs D continued. 'You play it' – she pointed at the speaker – 'too loud.' I saw her watching the man's chest and stomach. She shivered. Sparse black hairs grew along an almost perfect line above his nipples. Mrs Patel drew her children closer to her and the two West Indians introduced themselves.

Back down in my room I watched the ceiling and listened to the footsteps above me. The music began again soon after our departure, but this time only Mrs Patel reappeared to shout ineffectually through the closed door in a language no one understood – her revenge for all the complaints made against her. She encouraged her children to join her in an unsynchronized chorus.

Mrs D returned to my room during the afternoon under the pretext of checking that her warning had been successful. The music was still audible but, after listening to it for a few minutes, she said it was the best we could expect. They had no sense of decency, or right and wrong. She said that the Negro was not the man who had arrived to rent the room from her, as though this had some bearing upon her present failure. Then she asked me if I had any complaints to make regarding the Patels. When I said I hadn't she seemed disappointed. After the usual remarks about my work, she left.

I sat alone for the remainder of the afternoon and evening. At nine I put on my coat to go out, but decided against it. I went down to the front door and turned back. Mrs D's door opened an inch. She watched me and then the door closed. There were days, particularly in winter, when her own room seemed to contain the only warmth and colour of the entire house.

I encountered Mr Patel behind the counter of his small shop. He had already explained to me how much money was to be saved by letting the flat above the shop to his wife's sister and her family instead of living there himself. I shopped there often, but seldom for anything more than essentials. He told me where I might buy things cheaper. I said I ate very little and he patted his own stomach. Just as he did not bother to search each tin and packet for price tickets so he announced the total without looking down at his computerized till.

The small shop opened at eight in the morning and did not close until ten at night, often later. The cramped and colourful interior was scanned by a television camera, the picture projected on to a miniature screen above the till, where Mr Patel sat imprisoned for much of the day. Most customers he ignored, but some he watched closely, his face almost touching the screen.

Tonight he kept my attention by holding my change in his hand, settling it into a neat column with the same dexterity with which he calculated his totals and sorted coins.

'We are not a laughing people,' he announced unexpectedly. He emphasized the remark by waving a finger and pursing his wet lips.

Mr Patel's lips are smooth and pale and always seem to be about to burst and dribble water on to his chin. 'No, not a laughing people.' This time his tone was solemn. A street light cast the shadows of whitewashed writing on the window across his face, giving him the appearance of a New Guinea cannibal.

'No,' I said. 'I suppose not.'

'No,' he said. 'Indeed, very much the opposite.'

I remained uncertain of the significance, if any, of the revelation. If there was a point to what he was telling me, then I was missing it. After a short silence he climbed from his seat, pulled down the blind and locked the door. It was ten o'clock. When someone knocked he refused even to turn and explain, simply holding up his watch to them before turning back to me.

Before I could make any sense of the exchange, the plastic strips at the rear of the shop parted and out came Mrs Patel and her sister. They began to collect bars of chocolate from the displays. Mr Patel watched them and rubbed his fingers in a quick calculation. They addressed him in their shrill voices and he gave them money from the till, locking the door behind them as they went out. Then he laughed coldly, slid the change from his hand into my own, and said, 'They are going to Mecca.'

'Mecca?'

'Mecca Bingo. It is a joke.'

I said that I supposed it was.

'She wins non-stick pans at her first attempt,' he added sadly. 'Her sister checks her card. They miss a great deal, I think. Since the pans, nothing.'

'If I were you –'

'We are caught,' he said, almost shouting, patting himself on the chest. 'Caught!'

I understood even less of what he was trying to tell me, but the announcement seemed to cheer him up, as though it had been the point towards which we had been moving all along. He switched off his lights and held open the door for me.

Outside, I looked back and saw him outlined against the glow of his fridge. The shop and its contents looked like an abandoned and overgrown temple around him.

Atlas was explaining something to Farouk about a muscle in the small of his back. He twisted round and tried to look over his shoulder, directing Farouk's hand until the spot was reached. Farouk traced its outline with his finger.

'One of the hardest to manipulate.' Atlas raised an arm and grunted.

'It moved,' Farouk said.

Atlas smiled. 'Takes practice, steady work, building up. You ever consider anything in this line yourself? You look fit enough to have a head start on the rest of the flabs in the house.'

Farouk laughed. The last remark was made in a loud voice for my benefit. Through the keyhole I saw Farouk's hand remain in place. Atlas held his coat and jacket over his arm. There was another grunt and the skin rippled beneath the material of his shirt.

When I opened my door both men turned to face me. Farouk withdrew his hand.

Atlas said, 'We were just talking about muscles.'

'Makes a change.' I nodded back at Farouk.

Atlas frowned and put on his jacket. I rinsed my cup in the sink and struck a pose.

'You have muscles?' Farouk said. I wished he hadn't.

'Probably.'

He lifted and folded his own arms. 'We all have muscles.' He clenched his fists and turned them from side to side.

'It's what you do with them that counts,' Atlas said. He stuck out his chin and grimaced until the muscles in his neck stood out and the veins running over them throbbed.

'An obsession, you mean?' I said, and winked at Farouk.

Atlas deflated and watched us both suspiciously.

Farouk stuck out his jaw and felt his chin. 'Like this?'

Atlas nodded and reached out as though about to touch him. 'I could teach you. Come in handy would a bit of building, especially with your job.' He added the bit about the job deliberately to encourage Farouk.

'It would help,' Farouk agreed.

'The only problem,' Atlas went on, 'is jealousy. People get jealous. They see what you've got and think they should be entitled to the same.'

'That'd suit you, Farouk,' I said, meaning something different. He laughed and made an obscene gesture with his hand.

Atlas looked puzzled and then angry at being excluded from the joke. 'Any muscle you want,' he said. 'You name it.'

I nudged Farouk and he giggled. He pretended to think about Atlas's offer and was then unable to suppress his laughter.

Atlas acted as though it was all beneath him and told us to carry on. 'Perfection,' he said as we subsided. 'That's what you can't stand.'

Farouk touched himself on the chest to ascertain whether or not he was included in the accusation. He looked hurt.

'Perfection,' Atlas repeated. 'You've lost control over everything that happens to you. That's what you can't admit to.' He pointed at both of us. Farouk looked even more hurt and smoothed the creases from his jacket. Tonight the pattern was a kind of black and yellow tartan, with a black shirt and grey tie. We watched each other in silence, waiting for an interruption or diversion.

'There are men at the club,' Farouk said. 'They are muscle men. Bouncers. Big men.'

'Not always the same thing,' Atlas said.

'No. They are fat.' Farouk drew their stomachs over his own. 'Strong, but fat.'

'Intimidating,' I said.

He nodded.

'They're no better than –' Atlas began. He was going to suggest that they were no better than Farouk or myself.

'Gorillas?' I suggested. To further antagonize him, I said to Farouk, 'It's all a question of striking a balance between brain and brawn.' I knew as soon as I'd said it that I shouldn't have.

'Ah, yes,' Atlas said slowly. 'The freezing-garret syndrome.'

I tensed. Farouk, thinking a joke had been made, laughed.

The situation was defused by the arrival of Mr Patel on the landing. Our silence centred upon him. He commented on how smart Farouk looked. Farouk said something about his tie, rolling it over the backs of his fingers, pretending to be uncertain of it to encourage our compliments. Then he and Atlas went downstairs and I was left alone with Mr Patel.

'Soon be cold enough to snow,' he said, saying the words as though he'd already said them a thousand times to a thousand other people.

During the weeks following my arrival at Mrs D's I began to explore my new surroundings. The streets were composed mostly of Victorian houses with tall fronts and ornamental porches. Some had statues and designs built into the brickwork. In between these were terraces of smaller, later houses, the front doors of which opened directly on to the street. When the demolition work began these smaller houses were the first to go. They were also the easiest to clear, collapsing, it seemed, at the slightest push. Most of the larger houses had been converted into flats and spouted tangles of exposed plumbing along their backs. Most of their front gardens had been paved over and were filled with numbered dustbins. At the rear, the gardens had simply been allowed to overgrow.

On the first day of my exploration I walked as far as I dare without disorientating myself. I calculated my return via a different route and got lost. It was eight in the evening when I eventually found the street again. A group of card-playing Negroes sat on the steps to the house. I heard their laughter from my room, interrupted by long silences as they concentrated on their game.

At one end of the street was a small play area, and at the other, a cemetery – half overgrown, half immaculately kept with graves laid out in black and white slabs on a smooth green lawn. Above the entrance was a praying stone angel and, inside, a row of benches donated by grateful survivors. In the warmer weather I often spent my afternoons there with a newspaper or book.

On summer evenings the playground was full of children until well after dark. A man was arrested for exposing himself to a group of young girls and another for sleeping there and then verbally assaulting the first arrivals. Parents protested. The playground was locked and then the lock was smashed.

Beyond it was a petrol station open twenty-four hours and manned by a succession of teenage girls and older men. I bought cigarettes from the forecourt kiosk, and whenever I passed it late at night I returned the shouted greeting of whoever was on duty. It was in these small ways that I began to establish myself.

The petrol station closed down after a fire. The pumps were taken out and the kiosk boarded up. Someone wrote SORRY across one of the boards. The vagrants already 'resident' in the area moved in. Someone complained. The police returned. The vagrants went, returning months later when it no longer mattered.

In the overgrown half of the cemetery the graves were surmounted by crosses and life-size figures raising their hands and faces through the ivy which smothered them. Fat, decapitated cherubs stood in a chorus line over one spectacular tomb, each with a bow pointed heavenwards. Someone said that the tramps had gone from the graveyard to the petrol station.

I began to explore more widely. For very little money it was possible to ride a circular bus route for an entire afternoon. I knew my way past the playground into the city centre and out past the cemetery into the more distant suburbs, towards Lynette. I knew which of the local shops could be relied upon to fulfil a particular need, and then those which might fulfil it more cheaply. As my needs were reduced so my journeys decreased. During the autumn and first winter they stopped completely.

With the onset of the demolition, the spaces peripheral to my immediate surroundings came to represent a threat. The others said they felt the same. We became rabbits at the centre of a field of corn around which the harvesters had already started to cut. With the demolition of the streets between Mrs D's and the city centre I came to feel even more isolated and restricted in my movements.

By then the money I had taken with me from Lynette had dwindled and I was reduced to living entirely off the state. The speed and extent to which I became once again dependent on others was not something I gave much thought to. At the time it would have been the hardest truth to bear. Looking back, my initial period of readjustment was comparatively painless and short.

During those first months I collected a library of books from market stalls and second-hand bookshops. I walked on to the landing with a book under my arm. I cooked with one propped open above the cooker. When people asked what I was reading I told them it was rubbish and when it actually was rubbish I said the writer was underrated and misunderstood. I left books on the hall table with the intention that people should return them. When they knocked at my door I stood in the doorway rubbing my eyes, pinching my nose and looking pained. I gave the impression of having completed a hard day's work when in reality I had done nothing. It is something else I prefer not to look back on.

I acquainted myself with the bars in the neighbourhood. I drank. I became a familiar face and faces became familiar to me. I established a routine and kept to it. And when it ended, it ended slowly.

'Ice age,' Mrs D said. 'We're living at the start of the new ice age.'

'It certainly feels colder.'

It was her flimsiest excuse yet for entering my room. Only Mr Patel would have taken her announcement seriously. Her excuses were becoming flimsier generally. She waved the folded paper towards me. I was a Doubting Thomas. She was winning. Her proof. I asked her what she expected me to do about it.

'Nothing. There's nothing *any* of us can do about it. They've had them before.'

'They?'

She studied her paper. 'Thousands of years ago, millions.' The headline stood an inch high. 'You have to take these things seriously,' she said.

I told her I did.

'Extinction. The last time we all lived in caves.' She spoke about it in the same tone of voice with which she reminisced about her nights as a girl in the shelters during the war. The house was to be crushed beneath a massive wall of moving ice. She began to read. I asked her if she'd told the Patels. I was the first she'd warned. The seas were rising and the winter temperatures falling. I told her it didn't make sense. She said it made perfect sense and quoted the report of a combined team of American and Russian scientists. I wondered about the report's path from the learned journals to the paper she held.

'Russians,' she repeated, as though suggesting they were somehow to blame. In summer she blamed the short droughts on abandoned spaceships. It wasn't what she truly believed, simply an idea which appealed to her, and one she enjoyed repeating.

There was a crude map indicating the likely extent of the ice.

'We're well to the south,' she said.

I asked her if she knew anyone living in Hull or Manchester. She knew someone in Glasgow and observed a few seconds' silence for them.

At the slightest sound on either the stairs or landing she stopped speaking.

'It might as well be here tomorrow for all the difference it'll make,' she said. She laid down her paper and watched it unfold of its own accord. 'We never get what we want,' she added wistfully.

'A propos?'

'What?'

'The new ice age?'

She looked at me and sighed. Some of us didn't deserve to survive.

'That tap drips,' she said after a further long silence, pointing to the sink.

In the newspaper was a report of several dozen stranded dolphins and small whales. They had been washed up on the East Coast by an exceptionally high tide. Several of them, it said, had lain in shallow water and had died slowly over several days. Local people had sprayed them with sea water. Some had cut meat from the dead animals and fed it to their dogs. The dolphins looked like basking seals. Their plight. A pier had been badly damaged in a storm. It was all a long way off.

'And I don't suppose we ever shall – get what we want, I mean.' She created problems which she then resigned herself never to solving, none of which amounted to much more than the dripping tap.

She stayed for an hour. Columns of black smoke rose above the waste ground. Yesterday there had been a factory chimney on the horizon, today it had gone. She said she missed it but it hadn't even been visible until the demolition of the houses on the opposite side of the street.

'Everything will freeze up a long time before the ice actually arrives,' she said. 'It could be years. Everybody will have to migrate ahead of it.' She was reading from the paper again. She asked me if the maisonette she had been promised was north or south of where we lived now. I guessed at south.

The room grew dark around us. She avoided looking at the damp patch on the ceiling or at the pan of dirty water on the floor. A sister of her mother's had emigrated to Australia. Was that the same as migrating? It had only cost her a few pounds. It had been a land of Golden Opportunity. She'd seen brochures.

She asked me if I ever thought about dying. I confessed that I didn't. She said I ought to. I worried too much. I ought to be more like her. She'd been through too much to let something like a new ice age worry her. As fully as she appeared to enjoy her misery, so she was able to shed it.

The Patel children ran from one landing to another. She listened but said nothing. She wondered why people became so excited at the prospect of a few dead fish. 'Oh, no,' she said smugly. Correct her if she was wrong. They weren't supposed to be fish any more, were they? They were animals, like cats and dogs. They swam around in the sea, but they weren't fish. Was she right or was she right? It made as much sense as the approaching wall of ice.

In the newspaper was a cartoon: a crowd of wailing mourners gathered outside the shipping office after news of the sinking of the *Titanic*. At the back of them stands a man with a cloth cap holding a chain, attached to which is a polar bear twice his size. The bear is wringing its paws and looking anxious. The man is shouting over the heads of the crowd to the harassed clerk in the shipping-office window. 'Yes, yes – but is there any news of the iceberg?' There are tears on the polar bear's cheeks.

After our wedding I drank too much, got drunk and insulted Lynette's mother. She and Lynette were discussing the ingredients of the cake and I suggested we ought to mingle. Her mother said that her daughter had a mind of her own and that when she wanted to mingle she would mingle. Lynette, still in her dress but with the veil removed, calmed her down and said that her 'husband' was right. It sounded wrong even then.

I danced with Lynette, shook a lot of hands and built a small pile of presents, which Lynette and her female relations unwrapped and discussed throughout the course of the evening. Her father kept his distance, as did the other men, congregating around the tables by the bar. They told me how lucky I was and shared knowing looks.

Lynette's mother wanted a photograph of Lynette and myself kissing. Before she took it she had to find a replacement carnation for the one I had lost. We stood at the centre of the dance floor and listened to the disc jockey make inane observations about marriage and tell jokes about honeymoons. We smiled at each remark and applauded the jokes everyone else applauded. Lynette's mother returned and positioned our arms. 'Kiss her, go on, kiss her.' She crouched, held the camera, said 'Steady, steady,' and then straightened, complaining that the flash-bulb hadn't worked. Lynette looked uncertain. I said I'd had enough and left the dance floor. Her mother shouted for me to stay where I was. I ignored her. The best man put his arms around her, but she shook him off and said that her day had been ruined. Back at her table she began to cry, as much for effect as anything. When I eventually approached her to apologize she pushed me away and said that I'd started as I meant to go on. She said it loudly and proudly. Lynette sat with her and together they inspected the camera, as though by failing to work it alone had been to blame for what had happened.

The evening lasted into the morning. People arrived and left. The pile of presents grew and then decreased as individual items were unwrapped and passed around for closer inspection. It had become a rite of anitiation at which my presence was not essential. I stayed away.

Outside in the car park two departing cars collided and I went with several of the men to watch the ensuing attempt at a fight. Both drivers swung at each other, missed and fell over. Their wives remained in their seats, wound down the windows and started to chat. We helped the two men to their feet. They inspected the damage to their cars, admitted it was less serious than they had thought, shook hands and departed.

I waited outside in the cold air. Someone must have seen me alone and sent Lynette out to me. We stood together in silence, neither of us prepared to make public our uncertainties. She held my arm and said we'd both been under too much stress. She said her mother had asked her to apologize for her. I didn't believe her.

'I'm her only daughter.' It explained everything.

We were interrupted by a line of people dancing through the doors and on to the forecourt, singing and kicking their legs in unison. Seeing us together they formed a circle round us, closing in on us and then backing away. When the music stopped we applauded them and they applauded us. Then, feeling the cold, they ran back indoors.

'They're enjoying themselves,' she said. It seemed little justification for what was happening.

As we re-entered the bar she held my arm. It was late and the dance floor was full. The older men had started making fools of themselves. Lynette's mother sat alone. We went and sat beside her. She had been crying. When we asked her why, she said it was because she had never been so happy. She sounded as if she meant it and after a glance from Lynette I apologized for what I'd said and done earlier in the evening. Lynette smiled. Her mother smiled. We all sat around the small table smiling.

The disc jockey announced that the next record would be the last and that it was dedicated to Lynette and myself. We all danced. After that the wedding was over and everyone said their farewells and went.

At the end of the long rear garden is a narrow, walled alley and beyond that the gardens and backs of a parallel terrace, a mirror image. The distance is less than fifty yards. From late afternoon onwards, when the lights appear, I am able to watch a dozen small domestic scenes, mostly in silhouette.

I sit in darkness, certain of my own invisibility. The various functions of each room are easily identifiable and over the years I have observed a number of unvarying routines, of lights turned on and off in an order which almost suggests a prearranged sequence. The kitchens are the most rewarding to watch, but too often these are obscured by steam on their windows and by the continual departure of their occupants into other rooms.

I do not watch in the hope of seeing something unexpected or exciting, but simply to surround myself with the lives and daily routines of others. I have invented names for people, depending upon their repeated characteristics or the position of the windows at which they appear most frequently. Some couples argue every night; others move from room to room apparently without ever coming into contact with each other. I hear only the louder noises, and the voices only in summer when the windows are open. When it rains or when there is a wind, I hear nothing.

I have seen Farouk in the alley, leading his boys quietly down the garden, his palm pressed to their backs. He and I have reached a forced but acceptable understanding, and I cannot disapprove of what he is or does. He is an attractive man, and often both he and the boys wear black moustaches and have their hair neatly trimmed in identical styles. They wear the same colourful clothes. His own good looks have even disarmed Mrs D. She might suspect, but she does not know. She has even confessed to me that she considers it a great misfortune for him to have been born an Arab. Those were her words.

I dream. Only the minor details ever change. I dream and awake from the dream looking back at it. Some nights I am exhilarated, on others disappointed. 'Perfectionist,' Atlas once said, and it ended there. Small things like that. Mrs D pulls her clothes straight and asks if she is presentable. The ceremony began in winter and ends on a hot summer's day. Neighbours sit outside and raise their glasses to us. Striped canvas chairs are abandoned in favour of the cool grass of striped lawns. The vagrants sit with their legs open, like children on a beach. A pleasure steamer moves across the horizon, dazzlingly white and shapeless against a sheet of blue. Smudges of smoke remain imprinted on the sky behind it. The knife cuts and I hold it. Around us the house will be demolished. A high, brown wave races towards us and smashes through the downstairs rooms in a froth of foam and broken wood. Mrs D stands silhouetted against the window as she dresses.

The dream is no longer what it once was to me: there are too many superfluous incidents, too many others demanding a bigger role in the proceedings. Once, I half understood what it all meant, but not any longer. I am satisfied now simply to record its occurrence. Equally, I was once reassured by the precise sequence of events, but these have given way to variations on the theme of destruction, and as such are seldom duplicated.

Mrs D has collected a wad of envelopes from the hallway, each addressed simply to 'The Tenant' of each flat. Whoever posted them cannot have known our numbers. There are twice as many as required. Our individual anonymity is official, and something else of the mentality of the officialdom behind the envelopes is revealed.

The envelopes contain a mimeographed apology for the inconvenience being caused by the approaching demolition work and for our own forthcoming removal. There is a date, three months ahead. There are names and addresses to contact in case of difficulty or hardship. At the bottom of each letter is a rubber-stamped signature.

She had come to me because I was the only one likely to allow her to read what the letters had to say to us. The same illogical code which prevents her from entering our rooms without first knocking also prevents her from tearing open one of the surplus envelopes. She was behaving as though she might somehow now have the power to alter or influence the course of events ahead. The letters told us nothing we had not already known for the past year.

'Liberties,' she said. 'Everybody.'

I wondered if she meant us, or whether she was referring to the council for having written to us directly.

I showed her my letter. 'I doubt if it will make any difference to what happens to us,' I said.

'Not you, perhaps. But what happens to me when you lot have gone and the house is empty around me, what then?' She slumped into the chair at the table and looked ten years older in her defeat. 'They'll knock everyone down before they've finished.'

That was the general idea.

'I'd not kick *you* out, you know that,' she went on. She watched me to see if I was prepared to believe her. I saw her leading us like orphans through the mounds of rubble to a better place.

'We ought to get a petition up. Too late, I suppose. I could write to our M.P. Fat lot of good that'd do.' I doubted if she even knew who our M.P. was. I didn't.

It was late afternoon and already dark. I switched on the lamp beside my bed and the other on the table.

'Cosy,' she said, and made me regret the move.

She fanned out the remaining envelopes and said they'd arrived in the afternoon post. She was lying again: there had been no afternoon post since the demolition work began. All our services would be gradually withdrawn. A burst water-main had been cut off rather than repaired. Windows remained broken, patched with cardboard. Fittings were stolen. Occasionally the police arrived, shone torches from their cars into the empty houses and shouted to the men inside. They knocked on doors, listened, took notes of what had been stolen and went away.

'I've been to see the maisonette thing,' she confessed.

'And?'

'No key. I couldn't get in.'

'You should go. They might not always be so generous.'

'I know.'

I knew then that her resistance remained little more than a gesture of defiance.

'I should,' she said, suggesting I had convinced her of the benefits of the move. 'Fitted kitchens, they said. Wall cupboards, the lot. All painted and decorated.'

What were we compared to that?

'You've been here a long time,' she said.
'Too long.'
'I remember when you first came. A writer you were then.'
I began to speak. She touched my arm.
'What I meant was –'
I told her it didn't matter.
'No, I suppose not.'
I wanted her to leave.
'You've still got your books.' She waved her arm at the shelves in the semi-darkness.
'Yes, I've still got the books.'
She left the table and moved from one window to the other. 'What do you think I should do with all the other letters?'
'Leave them out. Let them collect their own.'
'What do you think they'll do?'
'There's not much they can do.'
'No, I suppose not.' She stood without speaking, looking out. It was almost as though something she had expected to happen in a year's time had been suddenly and unexpectedly brought forward to tomorrow.
'There's no real urgency,' I said.
'No, no urgency.'
I took my own letter and tore it in half. She watched and smiled. She came back to the table and took out her cigarettes. The room filled with smoke, adding to the illusion of warmth created by the dull glow of the lamps.
'You're the only one ever had lamps,' she said. 'None of the others ever bothered. Mrs Patel even had two fluorescent tubes fitted, Like living under a spotlight all the time in that flat. And all they ever did up in the attic was take out the ordinary bulb and put in a red one. You and me – we're the only ones ever had lamps.'
I wondered how much she was prepared to read into the connection. I said something about the light being relaxing.
'Exactly. Relaxing.'
The truth was that the overhead lights only made the room appear dirtier, sparser and colder than it already was.
'Neither of them' – she meant her husbands – 'could ever see the point of lamps.' She drew them out of the bag whenever she became maudlin or nostalgic, or whenever the thought of what was happening to her now compared to then depressed or disappointed her. She

counted out another half dozen of the envelopes and began to tear the remainder into pieces, one at a time, methodically.

'You might as well do it to the lot of them for all the difference it'll make,' I said. She shook her head. The code of conduct.

A year ago, when notice of the purchases and evictions had finally been given, there had been talk of a Residents and Tenants Resistance Group. But this had been quickly undermined by those who could not leave fast enough, and by those who felt too guilty to reveal their intentions of leaving until it was too late.

'Christmas,' she said unexpectedly, suddenly cheered by the prospect of something ten weeks ahead. 'We ought to all get together.'

I agreed with her and wondered how many of us would still be there in ten weeks.

Mr Patel shouted and knocked at my door. When I opened it he ushered me quickly across the landing and into his own room.

'There! There!' He jabbed at the television.

His wife knelt before it, her hands and face almost touching it. I thought at first that she had injured herself. Upon my arrival she moved to one side. 'We,' she said excitedly, pointing. 'We, we.'

On the screen was a picture of the street, half standing half demolished, and a reporter with a microphone talking into the camera. A progress report was being made on the redevelopment programme. They made it sound and look better than it was, and as though it was happening to someone else, somewhere else. The man told us nothing we could not have learned simply by looking out of the window or stepping out of the front door. I expected Mr Patel to announce that we were famous. The camera scanned the rubble and then the houses. At the appearance of our own, Mrs Patel squealed with delight and held her finger against it. There were a few figures in the street but we recognized none of them.

'We are in the newspapers and now on the television,' Mr Patel said. I told him it was an achievement. The report ended.

Mr Patel and I sat at the table. One of their small children lay asleep on the floor.

'There is to be a park,' he said. 'And a covered shopping centre with cafeterias and every amenity.' He said it as though he would have some part in it all, as though it wouldn't eventually put him out of business.

When the news ended Mrs Patel said something to the newscaster and turned guiltily to her husband.

'She swore,' he explained, and smiled down at her.

The following day I told Mrs D about the report and she asked me what the house had looked like on the television. I asked her why it should have looked any different and told her that the Patels had been excited at seeing it.

'It's my house,' she said.

I told her about the park and shopping centre and cafeterias.

There was never any reason not to suppose that Lynette and I would eventually part. She knew well before I did that I had become a liability and a threat to what she was trying to achieve. Everyone else had seen it all along. She began to use the word 'incompatible' in our arguments. It elevated them, made them worth fighting. The word suited her. She repeated it to her mother in self-defence. Her mother repeated it to me. It became a great argument winner. The rich and famous and glamorous became incompatible. They declared their incompatibility in the courts and on the television. It got them in the newspapers. And once adrift, I would reveal myself in my true colours. Never, in their opinion, was anything so certain. Predictions were made, glances cast. Alone, I would be nothing and it would be nothing more or less than any of them had expected.

The appearance of her mother on a regular basis aggravated matters. After the wedding I saw very little of her father. He seemed to regard our failure as the inescapable consequence of an all-powerful and rightful natural order. He had every reason to believe it.

The end was in sight when Lynette began to accuse me of upsetting the dogs, and then of frightening them. When she was out I went into the kennels and shouted and clapped my hands in front of their terrified faces. They bunched together in corners, forcing themselves into the mesh. On one occasion a terrier snapped back and caught my wrist. When Lynette returned I told her that the dog had attacked me for no reason. She knew I was lying and said so. I showed her the toothmarks. Then I made myself look ridiculous by accusing her of taking the word of a dog over that of her husband. She said, 'That's right,' and waited calmly for me to reply. I said she was sick. She said I was entitled to my opinion and knelt and called the terrier to her. It came and licked her fingers. When it saw me it growled and bared its teeth.

She smiled at the dog's reaction. 'They're noted for it,' she said. 'Tenacity.' It had become a selling point, something to be judged. 'Perhaps you should stick to stroking the poodle pups,' she said.

I accused her of being neurotic.

'My, my. How about pampered and over-indulged? But then that could refer to any of us, couldn't it?' She stared at me and smiled. She gave each of the dogs a biscuit and then offered one to me. 'Your trouble,' she said without looking round, 'is that you think you're something you're not. Even *you* can't deny that. And because you're not what you think you are now, you keep thinking that you'll become it tomorrow or the day after or the day after that. Some miraculous bloody hope. Well, you can wait at somebody else's expense. *We*'ve had enough of it.'

'We?'

'I – me – I've had enough of it. Me, personally. Me.'

The dogs sat and watched us. They always sat and watched us. I lost my arguments through them. They intimidated me.

I still believe, even now, that if I'd gone then I would have been back within a week, prepared to endure what was happening for a few months longer, years even. As it was, all I did was go out and get drunk. Upon my return I was sick in the kitchen and in the bathroom, and in the morning there were only damp patches smelling of disinfectant.

Her mother was there when I went downstairs. She held a bucket and cloth.

'Animal,' she said. She put a lot into it. 'Dirty, disgusting . . .'

'Animal?'

I scowled at her and forced her out of the house.

'Lynette's out,' she shouted back at me, as though that made any difference.

'She'll be filing for divorce' – blasphemy. She choked – 'I suppose. Unnatural practices and demands. Woof woof.' I watched her shiver at the thought. It rained lightly, and because she would not come back into the house while I was there, I stood at the kitchen window and saluted her with cups of tea. She left at lunchtime and Lynette returned shortly afterwards. She asked where her mother was. I said I hadn't seen her. She didn't believe me and to make her point she rubbed her finger across one of the damp spots and sniffed at it.

A man has started to paint a mural on the cemented end of one of the condemned terraces. It is intended to depict the variety and colour of local life. A dozen out-of-work teenagers are to be employed under the guidance of a single artist. The man has completed other murals depicting the variety and colour of local life elsewhere. Posters are exhibited. 'Our' mural is to cost the ratepayer nothing. Mrs D repeats this constantly and, of us all, only she is genuinely excited at the prospect of having the variety and colour of local life painted in twelve-foot-high figures for all to see on the wall of a condemned house from which all variety and colour have long since been driven out. That the building itself will soon be destroyed has occurred to no one. Some prefer to interpret it as a sign that the demolition work is nearing its end, that it might even cease before it reaches us; that it has become a machine out of fuel, an animal out of breath. Either way it is a useless and desperate hope.

The youths working on the mural spend their long breaks smoking and flicking the skins of dried paint at the tramps on the site across the road. A circular has been delivered asking for donations of any unwanted paints. Two of the youths stand beside a collection point and guard the few contributions. By mid-afternoon the wall is deserted. A simple scaffolding framework has been erected, and the upper half of the painting is hidden. When the artist leaves, people gather in the street to inspect his progress.

Above all, it is Mrs D who interprets the mural as an indication that our own terrace is to be spared. I point out to her that the painting is not actually on our wall. She retaliates by saying that it stands between ourselves and those houses already demolished. Few of the rest of us are prepared to be convinced that we are to be saved by a simple design composed of salvaged paint. The truth is that she continues to live in a state of permanent crisis and needs our agreement to convince even herself.

We have all inspected the painting, stood beneath it and looked up at the distorted figures beginning to take shape. The bottom of the wall is covered with graffiti and the ground is littered with stiff discarded brushes and empty cans. Mrs D tried to convince other householders that the painting would be their salvation. They are as desperate as she is to believe it.

There are days when no one arrives to continue the work and when speculation is rife about the project having been abandoned. Beyond the mural the demolition work continues.

The top of the wall is painted blue and white and dotted with doves and pigeons. Beneath the birds the horizon is filled with stylized trees and skyscrapers. Nothing exists on the skyline around it to identify it as local. There is an air of disappointment, of unfulfilled promise. It is beginning to look like every mural I have ever seen.

Mrs D continues to insist that we should be grateful for it. It is our gain: nothing, for once, is being taken away from us. We agree with her, but after the weeks of slow progress even her enthusiasm is beginning to fade. Cracks appear in the cement wall and are filled and painted over. Part of the recently painted sky is caught in a heavy shower and runs in streaks on to the outlined figures below. During the worsening weather, progress becomes even slower. There are days when it seems that nothing at all is added to the wall.

The first figure to appear is black, the second brown, the third white, the fourth a rosy pink. The faces are painted on round and oval blanks, and features are added later in lines of black and red. After a week of this more detailed work the realization dawns upon us that we ourselves have become the subjects of the painting. We are the varied and colourful local life.

I study each of the white and pink ovals for the beginning of my own face. Mr Patel announces that he has positively identified himself and takes us out in the half light to point out a figure in the middle distance wearing a white cap and flanked by two small brown children. For his sake we agree with him. Mrs D looks for herself but is disappointed. She resents her absence. She considers herself the mural's champion and feels cheated of what she believes to be her rightful recognition. There is a tall thin man walking a dog whom we all recognize, and a family of vividly yellow Chinese from the nearby take-away. They too have emerged to study the picture. The father poses a family group in front of the painting to take their photograph, handing the camera to someone else in order to be included himself. A few days later the photograph appears taped to the window of their shop.

I feign disappointment that I personally am not immediately

recognizable in the painting and then tense against someone disagreeing with me simply for the sake of being kind. No one does.

A few days later I watched Mrs D talking to the artist. She took something from her handbag and passed it up to him. He had more sense than to leave his ladder. She stood beneath him for half an hour. He took whatever she had given him and held it against the wall. The following week a woman began to take shape in the bottom left-hand corner. Her hair is blonde and her lips crimson. She is smiling and her eyelashes have been painted in thick black curls. She is wearing a red and white polka-dot dress and holding a black handbag. Her legs seem to bow at the knees and she looks about to fall over. Mrs D says nothing to any of us and cannot decide whether to be pleased or not at the result.

Before the novelty wears off, people still crowd to one side of passing buses to look. The stalls of a street market are added and most of the remaining spaces are filled with bunches of colourful flowers and anonymous faces. A red bus and a taxi are included and individual figures become less prominent.

'A remarkable likeness, no?' Mr Patel asks me, his relish of the obvious and clichéd remark undiminished.

'Remarkable.'

'And of the children too, no?'

'Particularly of the children . . .' His wife is not included. 'She is not local colour. Not colourful.'

I can neither agree nor disagree with him.

'It is a strange feeling to have oneself so prominently and permanently displayed in this fashion.'

I pay him the compliment he wants.

'And you – you are not disappointed?'

I tell him we cannot all be as fortunate as him and his children.

'True.'

All the black faces on the wall look identical and so the street is filled with happy and boastful blacks. The West Indians say that the black of the faces is too glossy and that individual features are difficult to make out. Mrs D thinks that there are too many coloured faces on the wall, that the area has been misrepresented. Mr Patel agrees with her. Atlas remarks that permission should have been sought before individuals were included. He himself is nowhere to be seen.

The mural takes two months to complete and is presented to The

People of the District at a brief ceremony dominated by the mayor and his wife.

Mr Patel came out of his room with two small glasses of clear liquid. He stood behind me and coughed to announce himself. His wife stood in the doorway beside him, smiling. He held the glasses between forefinger and thumb, gently raising and lowering them, waiting for my attention before speaking. Mrs Patel, I noticed, held a glass of orange juice. I switched off the cooker and turned to face them.

'A celebration,' he said. 'We have a new home.' He handed me a glass and tucked the thumb of his free hand behind his lapel. 'A new home.' He raised his glass to me and Mrs Patel drank her orange juice.

'Congratulations.'

He thanked me and drained his glass. I told him that I didn't think his religion allowed him to drink alcohol.

He looked at his empty glass. 'Alcohol? This? Pah.'

I drank my own. The liquid was bitter, but with no aftertaste. 'Non-alcoholic?' I asked.

He spoke to his wife and she brought out a small bottle. He read from the label, translated it, and said, 'See?' I told him I did and he refilled our glasses. His wife went back into their room, refilled her own and returned. From his impatience to continue and the way he stood I expected him to announce that they had decided to buy their own home.

'We are moving into the flat above the shop,' he announced. 'It is a very convenient flat and we will be very happy there.'

His wife said something and prodded him. 'Ah, yes,' he went on. 'It is fully carpeted throughout and with a spacious fitted kitchen. Many labour-saving devices.'

'What about your brother-in-law?' I asked. 'Are you moving in with him?'

'Him!' He frowned and said something to his wife. She made a deprecatory noise and laughed. 'No, no. *He* is moving *out*. He is there only temporarily as acting manager of shop in my absence. The shop is mine and it therefore follows that the flat is mine. We have discussed this with him and we have given him marching orders.' He smiled at the phrase, touched his glass against mine and emptied it again in a single gulp.

I said 'Congratulations' again.

'Yes. In order. And you yourself – you have found nowhere yet?'

I told him that there was no urgency, that the two months remaining was sufficient time.

'Ah, yes. Something will turn up, right?'

I said it would. For a moment I thought they were going to invite me to live with them. The second drink tasted even more bitter than the first. I sneezed and he laughed.

'A breadwinner has his responsibilities,' he said. 'It is only right that a growing family should have space in which to –' He stopped and turned guiltily to his wife. She watched him quizzically and then suspiciously. 'We – I – that is –'

'Is she pregnant?' It was more than a guess.

He turned to her and tried to smile. She said something to him and pulled a loose fold of her sari from her waist to her shoulder.

'A double celebration then,' I said.

'Ah, yes. The more the merrier.' He sounded unconvinced.

'You'll be glad of all that extra space.'

'Yes.' He poured himself a third drink.

I asked him if I should congratulate his wife. He looked at her, back at me, and left the question unanswered.

'Surely you must be happy at the prospect of another child?' It was something I had always taken for granted.

'Responsibilities,' he said. By then his wife had guessed what we were discussing. She shouted at him, then became girlish and whispered. He put his arm around her and spoke in the language they both understood. When he had finished she kissed his cheek and he raised his eyes to the ceiling, proud and embarrassed. I saluted her and lifted my glass for him to refill. I said I hoped they would be both very happy. It seemed to make more sense saying it to someone who didn't understand what I was saying.

'It is wrong time,' he said. 'Children are small happiness.'

I told him his own were the only ones I had ever known. This pleased him and he became more cheerful. He translated what I had said for his wife.

'When will your brother-in-law go?'

'Who knows? I have given him ultimatum. He has no choice.'

'Has something happened between you?' I said it through a smile for his wife's sake. She interpreted it as another compliment and bowed.

Mr Patel turned away from her. He rubbed his fingers together to indicate money. 'Sticky fingers, I think.'

'Is it serious?'

'It does not matter. We will move into the flat above shop and I will take on to myself the responsibility. It will mean more work, but . . .'

'Will you continue to employ him?'

He sighed. 'He is still family. He is husband of her sister. What else?'

'Will you be able to move in before Christmas?'

'I do not know.' He seemed less proud, less certain of his achievement.

'Have you told Mrs D?'

He shook his head.

'I'll mention it for you if you like. She'll be pleased for you – for the flat and the baby.'

'This is her home,' he said. 'All this. It was never ours. It will go like all the others.' He made his hands into a house and then flattened them, almost dropping his glass. Sadness seemed to be his natural condition. I wanted to convince him of his good luck, but he preferred to dwell on the misfortunes of others.

His wife spoke and he turned to listen to her. 'She says that she wishes you every success in looking for a flat of your own.'

I asked him to thank her for me and smiled at her as he spoke.

Atlas came down the stairs and stood between us. He said something about alcohol and muscle tissue. Mr Patel offered him a drink from his own glass. Poison. Atlas left us with his usual remark about us killing ourselves. We ought to be ashamed. I shouted after him that we were.

'*He* will find somewhere else to live very easily, you think.'

It wasn't a question but I nodded anyway. Mrs Patel said something and left us.

'She is no longer young,' he said as the door closed behind her.

I told him he was worrying unnecessarily. He said I was right, but shook his head. He lifted the bottle as though about to pour more drinks, studied the level of the liquid and screwed on the cap. I gave him my glass. I said I would help him to move his furniture when the time came. He held my arm and looked as though he was about to cry.

'I will tell her,' he said. 'Her sister will not speak to her. Do you understand what that means? She says money has spoiled us and made us forget what we are.'

I thought of his own cramped room and the long hours he worked and realized how unjustified the accusation was. I told him everything would come clean in the wash. I said it because I knew he would appreciate the phrase. He intoned it several times with his eyes closed and then went to repeat it to his wife. I had solved all their problems.

The tall Negro emerged to prepare a meal. It was the first time he or his girlfriend had used the cooker. I heard him shout to Mrs Patel through her closed door, demanding to be shown how the oven was lit. She ignored him, a fact made patently obvious by her silence after hours of noise. A minute later he knocked again, this time demanding matches. Again he was ignored. After that he banged on my door. I gave him a box of matches and followed him out. Every time either he or his girlfriend appeared, so did Mrs D, her door opening and closing in an echo of their own. I accompanied him in the hope of seeing the girl again.

After twenty minutes Mrs D climbed the stairs to join us. He watched her come up and then turned back to the cooker. In the oven was a shallow enamel dish. He watched it through the glass panel, pressing his palms against the warm door. The noise from the Patels' resumed.

Mrs D arrived beside us out of breath. She tried to make it appear as though we were not the reason for her visit. She passed us and then stopped and turned with a finger held up as though she had just remembered something. He ignored her. Even she did not know his name and was uncertain how to begin.

'Smells,' she announced, as though this explained everything (which it usually did – smells or noise).

I repeated it to add momentum to her slow start. She thanked me, assuming that I had sided with her; we were, after all, both white. The Negro stood upright and appeared even taller than he was. He wore a loose shirt which hung to his knees. On it were palm trees and crocodiles. Beneath it his legs were bare. On his feet he wore a pair of laceless plimsolls. From the knees down his skin was creamy, the colour of his palms. I felt suddenly intimidated, involved in something I should have avoided.

Mrs D folded her arms beneath her bosom. 'It has been brought to my attention,' she began. A variation on a theme. By saying it she wrapped her argument in what she believed to be unassailable logic and authority. It gave her confidence and a kind of security. She established a distance between herself and us. I was still a tenant, and never more so than in the company of the other tenants. She watched the Negro's legs as she spoke.

'There have been complaints about smells. From your room.'

The Negro smiled and knelt again to the cooker. I moved to stand beside his door in case the girl came out. Mrs D's arguments were defeated from the outset by the fact that the rent for the room was always paid promptly, and that apart from the attic rooms it was the smallest in the house. Before the arrival of the Negro and his girl it had often remained empty for long periods. I still found it difficult to believe that the two of them were able to live in it. It was twice the size of a double bed – an obvious measurement by virtue of the fact that half the room was taken up by a double bed. The ceiling was criss-crossed with nylon lines upon which they hung their clothes.

'You have a smell, man?' he said. I tried to decide how much artifice the sentence contained, and whether or not it was said deliberately to antagonize her.

'No. *You* have a smell!' She became angry. The crux of the complaint and argument had been forced into the open too soon. There were things she'd wanted to say which she would not now have the opportunity of saying.

'We all got smells,' he said. 'Now take Mrs Patel here. Her and her husband got smells that fill the whole house.' He crossed the landing and rapped again on Mrs Patel's door. 'That right, Mrs Patel?'

The instant he'd finished speaking she emerged to berate him. I retrieved my matches from the draining board and shook them in an attempt to suggest to Mrs D that they were the sole reason for my presence. We had all been aware of the smells from the Negro's room, and we were all – apart from Mrs D, I suspect – vaguely aware of their source. Mrs Patel continued to shout at him until her breath failed her. She hit him, stopped, and then backed away. The Negro laughed.

'You know what I mean,' Mrs D resumed. He ignored her,

turning back to the oven and his enamel dish. He took it out and lifted the lid. The smell was probably the sweetest the landing had ever known. In the dish were whole, unpeeled bananas and a pink mash of sugar and other fruits.

'Bananas!' Mrs D said, pointing. 'He's cooking bananas in the oven!' It became the final, damning piece of evidence in her favour. They were savages. Everything she had ever suspected was true. Mrs Patel peered into the dish, closed her eyes and breathed deeply. She said something to the Negro which suggested that she too was familiar with the dish. We were surrounded. Mrs D looked on unbelievingly, unable to accept that her argument and support were being lost because of the barbaric habit of cooking bananas in the oven.

Knowing that Mrs Patel would not understand, I said to Mrs D that it was an improvement on the smell of curry. My contribution was not appreciated. She glared at me. Allegiances shifted. I shook the matches again.

'It still doesn't alter facts,' said Mrs D. Another favourite – the 'facts' being the truth as she saw it. 'Smells are smells and there are things which no respectable –'

The Negro held out his hands towards her face. She stopped talking and plucked at her collar in a nervous gesture.

'Respectable – and –'

He touched each of her cheeks with his forefingers and then laughed at her sudden intake of breath.

'You too excited,' he said.

Mrs D rubbed her cheeks where he had touched her, studying her fingers.

'You don't want to let little things worry you. You got your blood pressure to think about.'

Her blood pressure was perfectly all right and none of his business, thank you. His accent and delivery sounded even more contrived than before. Mrs Patel said something, but no one listened.

'Who complain? Who say about smell?'

She was struggling for an answer when the two West Indians arrived to see what was happening. We could do very well without them. His victory was complete. They slapped hands and asked him what was wrong. He said, 'Nothing. Nothing wrong. Me and Mrs D here just having a little civilized conversation, that's all.'

I expected an indignant outburst from her at being called 'Mrs D', at being called 'Mrs D' in her own home, at being called 'Mrs D' in her own home by a banana-cooking savage. Instead, she told the West Indians to mind their own business and they left us, shouting down at us from the safety of their own landing.

'You ignore them, Mrs D,' the Negro said. 'Them all boys.'

She smiled uncertainly, her hand back at her collar.

He turned his attention once again to the enamel dish, dipping his finger into its liquid. We all flinched against the pain of the heat, but he simply smiled and licked it.

Mrs Patel licked her lips. Mrs D said, 'Yes, well,' and made the usual small gestures which signalled her departure. I moved to one side to let her pass. I doubted if the girl was going to appear.

'I save you some,' the Negro shouted down the stairs after her.

'Yes, you do that.' Savage.

He looked at me and winked. Mrs Patel waited for her own invitation. He offered, and from beneath her sleeve she drew out a spoon and took several large mouthfuls, pronouncing each one more delicious than the last by rolling her eyes and refusing to move away from the pan.

Nothing has yet been done about the leaks in the ceiling. I am expecting too much. Mrs D's own troubles are enough. They are too much for any honest woman to bear. Her troubles are our troubles. The leaking ceiling is nothing. The dripping water is nothing. The mention of them has become an insult. We know to expect nothing from her, but she insists we expect too much. Relationships are becoming much more finely defined.

I see her some evenings in several of the bars I frequent. I see her through the serving hatches between one room and another, surrounded by men, their heads wreathed in smoke. When I am drunk, it seems to me to be the only way she should be seen. Whenever I spot her I finish my drink and leave. Occasionally, however, when I am sober enough to be certain that I cannot be seen, I stay and watch her. She puts her arms around the men and kisses them. They inevitably try to take more than she is giving, holding her until she has to push them away. She disappoints me. Her Gentlemen Friends are drunks, measuring themselves only against her responses. Her attentions are all they receive, and in return they flatter her. It appears to provide the basis for a perfect, undemanding relationship. She seems a different woman in their company. That also disappoints me. She is no longer suffering. Worse – she is behaving as though the crisis has passed. She is drinking more heavily, spending more evenings away from the house. Seeing her with her arms around these men and drinking their drinks, I know that my leaking ceiling is the last thing on her mind. Watching her, I feel as though I am moving away from something I should never have released my grip on.

The barman sees me and turns to see what I am staring at. His cloth-covered hand moves round and round inside the same glass. It is a slow night, mid-week.

The room contains only a dozen other men. The drink is cheaper, but we pay for it in other ways. This room and rooms like it have become the only places outside the house in which I feel comfortable. The windows of frosted engraved glass give back blurred reflections. When he is not serving the barman stands looking into the other room. Music from a juke-box filters through. The man beside me begins to sing, but the words are those of a different song. He plays a piano on the table.

I can still see her through the smoke. A man is whispering to her and holding a glass beneath her nose. She laughs loudly at everything he says and caresses the side of his head, keeping his mouth close to her ear. Those around them have cleared a small space and are watching. She finishes her drink in a single swallow and hands the man her glass to refill. Some of the onlookers laugh and applaud her. A second man moves in to take the place of the first. He has a cigar, deliberately releasing the smoke in small spurts into her face. She blows it back at him. More applause. She slices her hand through the smoke as though clearing a path for her words.

The man beside me stops singing and begins a conversation with himself. He pays himself compliments and offers to buy himself a drink.

Later, sitting in the darkness of my room, I listen for the sounds of her return. Above me a television is turned on and there is the sound of running water, followed a few minutes later by the rising whistle of an unattended kettle. One of the Patel children is crying, and shining through the fanlight of my door is the light from their room. It becomes impossible to isolate individual sounds. An hour later the television is turned off and there is only silence. It has stopped raining, and because there is no noise I am able to sleep.

I stood with the two kennel-maids in the store room. They lit cigarettes and blew the smoke through the open window. The room smelt strongly of meal and biscuit. Lynette had nailed up two No Smoking signs after finding stubbed out cigarettes in one of the fire buckets. She lectured both girls on the possible consequences of their carelessness and they acted contrite. One of them stood by the door watching the house. I filled aluminium bowls with the grains and pellets from a line of sacks. I took the empty sacks outside and folded them in a neat pile. Lynette watched us from the house. It was raining and the dogs had been locked in their covered compounds.

The older girl flicked the moisture from her hair and swore. She accused Lynette of treating them worse than the fucking dogs. It was true. The dogs made her a great deal of money; anybody could be taught to feed them and then clear up after them. I wondered if I was included in the girl's complaint.

'I don't know why you stick it,' she said.

I wanted to tell her that I didn't, and that I cared even less for the dogs than they did. But I didn't: my explanations would not have convinced them, and when I went they would draw their own conclusions.

There had been no shows for a fortnight and none to come for a month. At the last, none of the dogs entered had been placed. Lynette had taken it personally. The woman whose dog had won had given her a photograph of the winning animal. Lynette showed it to me, demanded to know what it had that her dogs didn't have, and then tore it up. She allowed the dogs into the house and they followed her around. She picked up the ones which hadn't been placed and comforted them, as though they understood what had happened. The breaks between shows made her nervous. A lull arrived in the breeding season and she was convinced that some of her regular customers were staying away because her dogs had been seen to fail. The situation was worsened by the establishment of a rival breeder in the town and by the arrival of the circus.

The new breeder came to visit her a week after the building work on his own kennels had been completed. He told her he'd been breeding dogs for over thirty years. He inspected her kennels and made a point of showing surprise that they were constructed mainly of wood. He asked her if she didn't have problems with them during the winter. She said she didn't. He said she would. It had been a lie: she already did. Whenever he looked directly at her she smiled, and vice versa. I revelled in her discomfort. They sat together in the kitchen examining certificates. They compared their prices and achievements and Lynette told lie after lie. It was the first time I'd seen her behaving so insecurely where the dogs were concerned. After the certificates, the man inspected the small dogs which wandered in from the yard. He squeezed and prodded them until they yelped. He turned back their ears and held their tails flat across their backs, rubbing his fingers into the spaces between their legs. Lynette wanted to stop him, but said nothing. He invited her to visit his own kennels. He hoped they would get along well together. Lynette said that she was sure they would.

When he'd gone she called him a 'smug bastard' and then became angry when I agreed with her. She shouted at me, accusing me of not supporting her. Then she began to outline in detail what a rival breeder would mean in terms of her reputation and profits. She said that someone should have told her he was coming. I asked her if anyone was required to inform her. She looked straight through me and chased the dogs back out to the kennels.

The circus arrived during the weekend after her last show. The tent was erected on the waste land beyond the kennels and its perimeter ringed with caravans and generators. The noise lasted into the early hours of each morning, and the caged animals roared and bellowed until dawn. The small dogs became understandably restless. A string of coloured bulbs appeared above the wooden fencing and the noise of a television from a nearby caravan could be heard at all hours.

Lynette, predictably, complained. A letter from the council apologized and pointed out that she had been informed of the circus a month previously. She said she had not, and then found the letter unopened. She burned it and continued to complain. The council apologized again and said that there was nothing they could do. After that she went to the police and the fire brigade. Their answers were pretty much the same. She accused them both of not caring.

She said that everything was conspiring against her. I asked her what difference it would make to the dogs, their next showing being almost a month away. At the end of the week the circus would be gone. She hit me, not hard, but she hit me. She said that the other breeder had known all along that the circus was coming. I told her she was becoming hysterical.

The two kennel-maids had visited the circus and had told me in excited detail what they'd seen. They suggested I should visit the show. I said I might, but knew I wouldn't. The older girl said she wouldn't mind going to see it again. The other laughed and they exchanged an angry glance.

At the end of the week the circus went, leaving the waste land littered and churned to mud and water. Lynette rang the council to complain again. This time the man didn't even apologize. Instead, he asked her to put the specific nature of her complaint in writing and promised it would be dealt with through the proper channels. She hung up on him and swore at the phone for half an hour. I sat across the kitchen from her and watched her.

I told the two girls what had happened. Neither seemed interested. The older one asked me if I'd taken her advice and been to see the show. I said I hadn't. She said 'Thought not' and turned away. The younger one followed her out of the yard and into the store. I told them about the dog shows and suggested that they avoided Lynette as far as possible for a few days.

'She's still watching us,' the younger one said, looking out at Lynette through a space in the door. I said that we ought to go into the kitchen and wait for it to stop raining. They said they'd prefer to wait where they were. The older girl asked if Lynette and I ever went out together. I said that there was seldom any time. She asked me how long we'd been married and laughed when I told her. The four years sounded like forty.

My dream of killing Mrs D continues. It has begun to recur more frequently, and has been extended to include the Negro and his girl, Atlas and Farouk. The Negro stands above Mr Patel, who continues to hold down Mrs D's head and shoulders, and waves his arms. He is wearing only a loin-cloth and, around his neck, strings of white and yellow teeth. His body has been rubbed with oil and shines. The girl stands beside him in her white sheet, watching and moaning. Mrs D neither struggles nor screams, and I am still the one with the knife. Atlas and Farouk simply watch the Negro and cheer each slash of the knife.

On several occasions I have awoken before any cuts were made. On another I halted the proceedings and released her. Everyone moved away but she refused to stand. She looked up at each of us, disappointed.

I awoke an hour before the late dawn. The moving shadows and light of a fire in one of the empty houses shone against the window and over the ceiling. I lit a cigarette and sat upright, exposing my arms and chest to the cold air. The house remained silent. From outside came the noise of shifting rubble. At the top of the house someone coughed violently and the sound filtered down through every wall and into every room.

In the previous week there had been two new arrivals, both from the demolished houses of a neighbouring street. One was an Irishman who described himself as a construction worker and brought with him nothing but a canvas bag of heavy tools. He is known simply as 'the Irishman' and his Irishness is the most obvious thing about everything he says or does. He makes it obvious. He breaks his sentences, turning statements into questions and vice versa. Like the rest of us, he plays a part and is comfortable within it. When we do not wish to refer to him as the Irishman, we simply call him 'Irish'.

The second new arrival was a man in a suit who carried a rolled umbrella and square black briefcase. Everything about him was shabby. He left the house punctually at eight and returned punctually at six. He was too methodical and precise to be anything but a fraud. When it was raining, he returned wet, looking exhausted and with splashed mud on his trousers. He told Mrs D that he had recently started a new job and that he had been forced to come to it ahead of his wife, children and belongings. She sympathized with everything he said and then repeated it all to me.

Both new arrivals pay their rent weekly instead of monthly. It is a small sign, but one which the rest of us cannot ignore.

To Mrs D, the man in the suit was another of her Gentlemen. The title satisfied and pleased them both, making something out of nothing and disguising the truth without actually making it a lie. She has invited him into her room on several occasions. Everyone with an opinion on him mistrusts him. Farouk suggested we should tell her he was a council spy, there to undermine us. The idea was rejected. Atlas said he didn't understand why we were all so concerned. (He still considers himself apart from us. When the day comes he will flex his muscles and fly away. The rest of us will disappear.) Farouk said the man's face was familiar. But it is something he says too often for it still to have any real meaning. He believes it makes him appear more important. He enjoys being the centre of attention, and I cannot understand why he does not feature more prominently in the dream.

I have seen the Irishman in several bars. He is the kind of man who is able to be both uncontrollably drunk and then politely sober in the space of a few hours. He wears a cap and always raises it to Mrs Patel and Mrs D. In the bars he is surrounded by other Irishmen and by old Negroes wearing plastic fedoras. I know precisely how Mrs D would respond to him if she met him outside the house. At nights he sings on his way home. His voice carries well through the empty streets, but by the time he reaches the front door he is silent. He is the kind of man who would sleep in his clothes.

My arms and fingers are numb from the cold and I wonder if I am making an unconscious effort to wake from the dream and prevent it from reaching its conclusion. I feel as though I have been shown a glimpse of something and then had it taken away from me. Some mornings I awake from it feeling as though I have committed and then regretted an act of betrayal.

Four years ago there was a suicide in the house. It happened in one of the rooms directly beneath the attic. A recently arrived tenant hanged himself from the light fitting at the centre of the ceiling. The weight of his body tore out the wiring and fused the lights in the entire house. The fuse boxes were checked and the fault traced. Getting no reply from the room, Mrs D opened the door with her master key. The room looked untouched since the man's arrival. On his bed lay an open suitcase. He had fallen and then slumped to a kneeling position, his head bowed forward, his palms resting on the floor. He looked as though he might be about to do a handstand. Someone from the third floor arrived with a camera and took several photographs of the body before someone else remarked upon his actions being distasteful.

Mrs D pushed the suitcase from the bed and straightened the cover. I suggested to her that we did nothing until the police arrived. She agreed and studied the wiring which dangled from the ceiling.

She asked me if I thought it was unsafe. 'Poor man,' she said, studying the bare room around him, commenting more upon his situation before his death rather than his death itself. Someone found a Polaroid photograph of the man with his arms around a woman wedged behind the mirror above the sink. More pictures were found in his suitcase. Other tenants began to make remarks about that kind of thing happening every day, about the inevitability of it happening here. Someone said that the house itself had a bad influence on some people. Mrs D knelt beside the dead man and wanted to be able to say that things like that didn't happen in her house.

The police and an ambulance arrived. We were ushered away and then interviewed individually. We confused the issue with our speculations and guesses. All they needed to know they took from the man's wallet. We all stood at our doors watching the covered body being manoeuvred on a stretcher down the narrow stairs. Afterwards, the man who had taken the photographs offered to sell me one. He discussed the possibility of selling them to a newspaper.

Mrs D arrives on the landing with the news that today was the anniversary of her first husband's death. She said she'd thought a lot of him, and that on balance he'd been a better husband than the second. She told us how old he would have been. She'd taken down his photograph and turned that of her second husband to face the wall for the day. The Irishman said that it seemed the only decent thing to do. He asked her if she intended celebrating the occasion. She said the thought hadn't occurred, but that it was what he would have wanted. He'd been a drinking man. The Irishman smiled. Mr Patel contributed to the conversation by announcing that his parents had also been dead for a similar length of time. She said she didn't see the connection: they'd died in India and it was hardly the same thing. Her first husband had been an educated man, had had two men under him in the Parks Department. Mr Patel conceded the argument. She said that we ought to have seen him in his uniform, that he looked like George Raft in *Each Dawn I Die*. Had any of us seen it? None of us had.

'And was it the drink?' the Irishman asked.

She shook her head and sighed. 'Dicky ticker.'

'Ah.'

'He was in charge of all the flowerbeds, the floral clock and bowling greens.'

'Too much for him?'

'In the end. They offered him a job in the hot-house, but he was always an outdoor man.' Had we seen George Raft in *Spawn of the North*? None of us had. It was how he'd looked.

Mrs Patel said 'Dicky ticker', and repeated it over and over until it came to sound like a character out of *The Jungle Book*.

He'd been taken in his uniform. It was what he would have wanted.

'Dikkitikki.'

Mrs D watched her suspiciously. It was better than being eaten by a tiger or stepping on a snake.

I hoped for her husband's sake that Mrs Patel would say no more. She did, but nothing any of us understood.

He'd been buried in his uniform and there had been flowers from the hot-house on his grave. A guard of honour, other gardeners, hoes instead of swords, another sigh at the memory.

The Irishman said he sounded like a fine man and that he'd celebrate with her. She thanked him. She said that when she'd realized the date she'd cried. None of this would be happening to her now if her first husband had still been alive. Naturally. He'd taken a great pride in the appearance of things. It was only after he'd gone that she'd had the small front garden cemented over. She listed the plants which had been uprooted or buried. Now only grass grew between the cracks. Her second husband had done his best with the garden at the back, but only to please her. It had deteriorated rapidly under his care and he'd suggested on *his* deathbed that she had it covered over too. He'd said a great deal on his deathbed. In fact he'd had something prophetic, revealing or damning to say about almost everything on his deathbed. In truth, I was tired of hearing of him. He bored us all from beyond the grave. He'd said an Englishman's home was his castle and had then recovered sufficiently to explain what he meant. He'd said that an Englishman had the right to work at whatever he chose, but had worked himself for only a month of the decade the marriage had lasted. From what I'd heard of him he'd brought nothing but himself to the marriage and had drawn upon it continuously until he'd died. He, too, had been a drinking man.

I pointed out to her that her second husband seemed to have spent an inordinate amount of time on his deathbed talking.

'He was a long time dying.' A look: don't speak ill of the dead.

'In fact he seems to have gathered all his bons mots into a kind of overall, final philosophy.'

'He had a very active mind.'

'He was supposed to be dying!'

'Not of an active mind he wasn't.' Victory. She folded her arms.

'What was it then?' the Irishman asked.

His insides. She mouthed the word. 'They were never very specific. He'd had it a long time.' She'd been with him ten years and had done all she could. No one could blame her. He'd been comfortable and happy. His anniversary came up in a month. The Irishman said he'd help her celebrate that too. She said he was the only one of us with any compassion. We all had to die. Some sooner than others. Came to us all in the end. And when we'd gone – she hoped no one would speak ill of her – we'd gone.

Mr Patel announced that his father had been eighty-eight and that he'd walked ten miles to and from work for almost seventy years. But that had been in India, a different thing entirely.

If they were going to celebrate, the Irishman said, then . . .

They descended the stairs together.

There is a slender gap beneath the almost continuous cloud through which the sun rises and then sets. In the morning it is reflected into my room from one of the lower windows of the houses to the rear – a distinct orange ball which passes over my bed and across the opposite wall. It lasts no longer than twenty minutes and the light is more artificial than natural. For those few minutes I might easily deceive myself into believing that the room was warm. Even the shapes of my breath in the cold air do little to dispel the illusion. It might even be early on a summer's morning.

I lie awake, watching the sun's progress and listening to the noises of the people around me. The Patels are always the first up, using the bathrooms on each floor before anyone else is ready. Even their two small children are up and dressed at seven.

There were mornings soon after my arrival when the waking thoughts of what I might achieve on each day became an almost unbearable pain. For weeks I made a last determined effort to work, to sit down and write. And then I began to search out and familiarize myself with the house's distractions. It was a routine to which I became quickly attuned. I achieved nothing and was aware only of the contrived nature of everything I did. I considered myself in a sort of limbo. It was what, in the end, persisted and defeated me.

The sun slid over me and fell to the floor prior to its ascent of the wall. I knew to the inch the path it would follow. Given sufficient time its course will be marked by a curve of faded colours.

Below me Mrs D is awake, tuning her radio and moving from her room to the front door to collect her milk. Someone crosses the room above me and water begins to move through the pipes. Mr Patel will be the first to leave, followed by Atlas and the Irishman, followed by his children.

More rain is forecast. My breath still clouds the cold air. The sun climbs the wall, loses its brilliance, and fades to nothing.

Lynette had been away for the weekend at a show and I'd spent Saturday night on a couch at the last of our friends, the wife of whom had been in hospital giving birth to their third child. I stayed with the husband who was alone in the house. He drank too much and fell asleep in the chair beside me. At four in the morning someone rang to say that the baby, a third girl, had been born at ten minutes past three. His wife had been asking for him. I thanked whoever it was and tried to rouse him. He awoke. I told him. He cried and said that the kids had destroyed him. I said it was the same with the dogs. He said I didn't know what I was talking about, got dressed and drove us to the hospital. We spent the rest of the night in a corridor. Later he apologized for what he'd said. I told him he was right and that it didn't matter. After that night we never saw each other again.

At the hospital reception desk he demanded to know why he hadn't been told until almost an hour after the event. The nurse looked at him accusingly and I helped him back to his seat. He swore and said he could manage by himself.

I left the hospital at eight in the morning and walked home. I could hear the dogs from the end of the street. They had been left unattended all night and I would have to spend the rest of the day cleaning them out before Lynette returned. She would probably have rung some time the previous evening with news of the show. Two of the dogs were fighting and one of them already had a scratch on its muzzle. They were both males and so no more permanent damage would have been done. I swept them out, fed and watered them.

I wanted to spend the afternoon writing but was too tired. I sat at my desk, counted the finished sheets and realized how little I had done in the previous months. There had always been something else: the dogs, her, the house, the kennels, anything.

When she returned she spotted the injured dog almost immediately. I acted surprised and pretended I hadn't noticed. She said calmly that I was lying and that it was no more than she expected. The dogs she'd taken to the show sat in their baskets on the table. I asked her how they'd done.

She said, 'Two places and two breeding appointments.'

I said, 'Well done.'

The dogs watched us. I picked them up and carried them into the kennels. I told her about the hospital and the baby as she bathed the injured dog's cheek. She replied disinterestedly that she'd send a card.

I left her and went back into the house. The third-time father rang. I said I'd told Lynette about the birth. She came in and took the phone from me. She was thrilled. Everyone was so happy. She said it without any visible emotion, but it sounded right. What were they going to call it – her? The man remembered to ask about the dogs. She asked him who wanted to talk about the dogs at a time like this . . .? How was his wife? I waited beside her. She said I was waiting to talk to him. She wished everyone well and said she'd visit them soon. She handed me the receiver and left. The man and I said little to each other that we hadn't already said the previous evening. He apologized again for his behaviour and for what he'd said about the children. I heard them behind him, shouting through a closed door. He could think of nothing else to say and the earpiece filled with the noises of the house around him. All *he* would have heard would be the barking of the dogs. He said he had a list of people to ring. He started to say something to one of his daughters and then hung up.

Lynette went outside and then reappeared with the injured dog, sitting with it on her lap in front of the television. She informed me of a show in a fortnight's time for which she would have to be away from Friday until Monday. She asked me if I could be trusted to look after the dogs, or whether she ought to invite her mother to stay. I said it hardly mattered, because if her mother came I would go. She relented reluctantly.

The following morning she instructed the two kennel-maids on the care of the injured dog. Then she went out. Before she left they took a dog each and began to brush them. Whole curls of white hair fell on to the table. At the sound of Lynette's return they gathered these up and dropped them hurriedly into the bin. I asked Lynette where she'd been. Her reply was a suspicious glance at the girls. She said she preferred not to discuss private matters in front of the staff. The older girl stopped herself from answering back. Lynette stroked the two dogs, rubbing their coats and inspecting the palm of her hand. She said that one of them needed shampooing. The girls took the dogs out. When they'd gone, she said that neither of them was any good. I asked her if she meant the dogs. She said I knew precisely what she meant.

In the late afternoon she went to see the rival breeder. He had written with details of a bitch in breeding condition for which no suitable dog could be found. I asked her about it when she returned. She said she had a dog but that the man could go to hell. The more names she called him the happier she seemed. She was clearly worried at the loss of her hitherto unchallenged monopoly. I pretended to sympathize with her and said things about the man and his dogs which were really about her and hers. When she finally agreed with me, my own small victory was complete.

During the day a gang of workmen have erected the timber scaffold of a poster hoarding, ninety feet long and thirty high, looking down over the derelict land opposite us. The Irishman, who assured us he knew about such things, said it was common practice. He asked Mrs D about bus routes, made a calculation and informed us that when the hoardings were completed, the posters would face towards us. I told him I thought it unlikely. He said I was entitled to my opinion and winked at Mrs D. She winked back. I knew where I stood. A few days later the hoarding was pasted with three large posters looking towards us. Only Mrs D bothered to point out that I had been wrong and the Irishman right. The two outer boards advertised supermarkets in bold black and orange lettering. Between them stood two heavily tanned women wearing wet-suits and advertising rum. Water dripped from their arms and legs, and their lips shone and were open in perfect circles. One of them held a trident upon which a fish was impaled. Behind them was the white beach and perfect blue sky and sea of the Caribbean. Mrs D made her feelings about the poster known to us all before the men had finished piecing it together. I said it could have been worse. She asked me how. I eventually agreed that it was in bad taste, especially in view of what was happening to the neighbouring streets. When had any of us ever had the opportunity to visit the Caribbean? Farouk said it reminded him of home. Mr Patel, ensuring that a closed door lay between us and his wife, said he thought the two women were fine and colourful and showed that someone still cared. I was uncertain exactly what he meant. I remarked to Mrs D that it reminded me of something in *The Great Gatsby*. She said he sounded like a club act. Or was he a woman?

At night the hoardings were partially illuminated by the street lights which still remained between them and us, and in the darkness the women's dark faces looked paler, their eyes vividly white.

Yesterday I inspected the newsagents' windows again. Single Gentlemen, it seemed, were still preferred. I collected telephone numbers and addresses, each of which I located on a street map and marked with a cross. The map became proof of my willingness and ability to respond to the situation. In one window there was still a card advertising the empty rooms at Mrs D's.

Mrs D saw my map and became immediately anxious. She said I was her best tenant and practically accused me of being about to desert, abandon and forsake her. I told her she was over-reacting. She asked me what the others would do when they saw me leaving. I told her that I had to be realistic. She relented grudgingly and said she supposed I was right. I reassured her by telling her that none of the rooms I had so far seen came up to the standards of the one in which I now lived. Only she would have been prepared to believe such an obvious lie. There had been no other rooms. She responded to my flattery as though she believed we all lived with her in the greatest comfort and luxury, and that we did so solely as a result of her own unselfish efforts. She asked me if any of the others had started looking.

Earlier, Mr Patel had stood on the landing and become philosophical. He said he was relieved that the final date was drawing near. Living with it far ahead, he said, had bred false hope – hope that external influences might yet gain us a reprieve. I said he was right. He sighed and said, 'Six weeks.' I asked him if his brother-in-law had vacated the flat above the shop yet. He shook his head. If the worst came to the worst, he said, they would all live together. Wouldn't they be very crowded, I asked. He sighed again and said that everything was relative. I wondered if he'd made a joke, but saw by his unhappy look that it was unlikely. I showed him my map and he said I was right to have a plan of campaign, that a good plan would result in positive action. I told him that he was being profound. He said, 'Probably.'

Atlas arrived and said he couldn't see what all the fuss was about. I am beginning to wonder if his interruptions are entirely coincidental.

'Six weeks,' I reminded him.

'So?'

A few minutes later Farouk arrived. He listened intently to what we each had to say on the matter before expressing the opinion that we were all right.

'Typical,' Atlas said.

'Positive action,' said Mr Patel. 'A good plan –'

Atlas interrupted him, saying we were all behaving like old women. After that he left. He passed the Irishman coming up the stairs who greeted us all loudly and showed us a bruise he had sustained at work, as a result of which he had been given the remainder of the day off. He knew a bar which stayed open all afternoon. He kissed the bruise and left us.

The following day I went to see my first flat. The card had appeared in the window of the Chinese take-away, written both in Chinese and bad English. The man who answered the door didn't even speak bad English, only rapid Chinese, which he delivered in short bursts, screwing up his face and stopping unexpectedly as though in pain. After each sentence he looked at me quizzically. When I pointed to the card he shouted into a back room and a woman appeared. He spoke to her and she studied me. She then said that they were hoping to let the room to a Chinese girl, that that was what the advert said. I was not a Chinese girl. I said I understood her disappointment, but that the wording of the advert had not made this point very clear. She spoke to the man and they both watched me suspiciously.

'Chinese girl,' he said. The effort seemed almost too much for him.

'Someone to serve in shop,' she explained.

I said that I understood and apologized for having wasted their time. I was about to leave when another, much older woman appeared and spoke to them both, her eyes never leaving me. They explained to her that I was not a Chinese girl. She laughed and waved her hands at me. I told them I would still be interested in seeing the room. I followed the old woman up a flight of narrow stairs and into a room directly above the shop. The walls were painted pale blue, the ceiling and woodwork yellow. The only decoration was a large calendar from which a line of identical Chinese children grinned down. From the centre of the ceiling hung an ornamental lampshade made of paper and cane and with silk tassels. The old woman switched on the light, climbed on to a chair and spun the shade, pointing excitedly at the brightly coloured birds and dragons through which the light shone. The man entered the room behind us, saw the old woman on the chair and shouted at her. The old woman ignored him, mesmerized by the spinning shade and the patterns it cast over her face. I said I didn't think the room would suit me, but none of them seemed to understand. The younger woman looked offended. She pointed to the room's three chairs and then sat on each, inviting me to do the same. She patted the bed and turned on the taps in the sink. The room smelt of fried meat. She opened a window. The old woman scolded her and demanded to be helped down from the chair. She ushered us all out of the room and back down into the shop. The man became exasperated and shouted at her. The younger woman calmed him. I was uncertain as we stood together in silence whether or not they believed I was going to take the room. Eventually the man spoke and the younger woman translated.

'It is her room,' she said.

'Is?'

'Was. It was her room. She live downstairs now. She has bad fall.' She patted her thigh. 'Very old.' She lowered her voice, as though the old woman might understand what was being said. The shop too smelt of fried meat and stale oil.

'Chinese girl,' the man said.

The younger woman looked uncertain. 'They knock all down very soon anyway,' she said, running the words together until they sounded Chinese.

When I understood what she was saying I asked her why they had advertised the room if they did not expect to let it. She shrugged and nodded to the old woman.

'She has been here twenty years. I was a girl.' It probably made a great deal of sense, but not to me. The man moved closer and put his arm around her. I apologized again for having wasted their time. All three stood in the doorway and waved as I left.

When Mr Patel asked if I had been successful, I told him that I hadn't been able to see the room.

'Ah, yes, Chinese,' he said.

Paradoxically, as the time grew shorter our sense of urgency seemed actually to decrease. The simple truth, I suppose, was that we had resigned ourselves to what was going to happen and no longer believed in our ability to do anything about it. In a sense we had been relieved of an obligation and no longer felt compelled to make public our various inadequacies.

A group of gypsies have moved on to the cleared land beyond the terrace to the rear. After only a few days they seem to have been there for ever. Both they and the vagrants consider themselves above the other and, as a result, the two groups keep well apart. Their caravans and lorries are drawn into a semi-circle and their fires burn day and night. They are surrounded by thin dogs and thinner children, and possess two off-white horses, tethered and moving constantly in a circle in search of grass. There is already graffiti telling them to leave on the concrete pillars of a nearby fly-over. The men sit on crates around the fires with air rifles. They frequent the bars and remain together, small, black-haired and brown-faced in dirty suits. Our suspicion of them is largely instinctive. The women make a living by selling household goods which no one really wants from door to door.

They knocked at our door and Mrs D stood in the hallway with a finger to her lips, the other hand pointing to the broken outline of the woman through the glass. I asked her what was wrong. She waited until the woman had gone before speaking.

'Gyppos.' There didn't seem to be any way of saying the word without making it sound hard or cruel.

I said I doubted if a curse on us all would make too much difference.

They were still gyppos. She'd been brought up in fear of them. I didn't understand.

'Powers.'

I told her I thought she was over-reacting. Lucky heather, songs around the camp fire, the open road, gaily painted –

I could believe what I wanted. None of this would have happened a year ago when the council still cared what happened to us. We still paid rates. Why should it happen to us now? She asked me to go to the door and check to see that the woman had gone. I went. She had.

'Good.'

She drew on her gloves. They'd be in and steal the silver given half a chance.

'What silver?'

Oh, I'd be surprised.

I asked her if she was going out. She was. I walked with her, making a detour to avoid the encampment. A gypsy had read her mother's palm and less than a month later she was dead. An infectious disease. At a seaside parlour, all lace and half-light and fading newspaper cuttings of the rich and famous who'd held out their own palms. None of *them* had died. Case proven. I told her we were likely to be gone long before they were. There was no justice in the world.

I asked her if she'd been serious about her mother. It wasn't something she'd joke about. Her mother had been ill for years. She'd been to the fortune-teller because the doctors had only repeated their diagnosis. There had been no mention of a death in the family at the sitting.

When we returned the fires around the caravans were burning high. A woman sat plucking a chicken and scattering the feathers into the air. The dogs barked at our approach and were shouted into silence.

They were beggars, thieves and murderers. Ask anyone. I wondered if anyone within a half-mile radius wouldn't have said precisely the same. We were scapegoats passing on a scapegoat's luck.

Several days later a pig appeared at the encampment. A letter was printed in the local paper saying that the proper place for pigs was the country. Someone else wrote to say that pigs belonged in pig sties. The pig stayed. They fattened it on garbage and a week later it was gone. I remarked on the fact to Mrs D and she drew a finger across her throat and made a gasping sound. It confirmed everything she'd said. Butchers. She wouldn't put anything past a gypsy. She even accused the Irishman of coming from a country where they were encouraged. He asked her if she'd ever been to Ireland. She told him not to try and change the subject. Everyone knew where they came from.

Ah, yes, but –

Ah, yes, but nothing. Deny it.

Well – pause – as a matter of fact –

As a matter of fact nothing.

Ah, but taking into account –

She told him he'd lost the argument. He was perfectly safe up on the third floor. She, on the other hand, slept at ground level. She drew another finger across her throat. Her and the pig. He saw her point and his argument left him in a sigh.

Two days later the pig was back. It had escaped. This time it was tethered by its foot to a post. The younger children rode on its back.

So the pig was not dead and the argument resumed. A different pig, she said. Stolen, no doubt, he said. No doubt. She wrung a second victory from the same argument.

She said that for the first time in years she'd dreamt of her mother. The Irishman asked her what it proved and she called him callous and uncaring.

I watched the pig one day and cannot remember having seen anything, animal or otherwise, looking at once so utterly content and so utterly miserable. It moved over the rubble on its short legs like an ungainly mountain goat and then sank like a pink boulder into the liquid mud at the centre of its own small world. It even starred in a cameo appearance with Mrs D's mother in the dream.

They were at the seaside and as her mother came out of the fortune-teller's booth the pig had passed in front of her, almost causing her to fall. The pig seemed not to have noticed, and thereafter reappeared intermittently, often only in silhouette, throughout the remainder of the dream which by then had been completely spoiled.

A week later the pig disappeared again, this time never to return.

Mrs D hoped her own end, when it came, was as swift and clean. Her mother had gone rapidly downhill after the seaside visit, and thereafter had persisted against all odds. She had been a saint. There had not been a woman alive who deserved less to die. The Irishman said 'Ay-men'.

The gypsy men sold the bacon in the bars. People bought it wrapped in newspaper – not because it was any cheaper than that in the shops but simply because it was what men in bars did. Mrs D herself bought tights and scent in bottles without labels. But that, of course, was different.

'Ay-men.'

To that.

They'd be in that night to slit her throat.

Oh no they wouldn't. Not her.

We left her. She shouted 'You'll see!' up the stairs after us. We would. No doubt about it. None. History repeating itself. Dead within a month.

And then what? And then where would we be without her?

Contrary to my pessimistic predictions, the completed mural has remained standing and largely intact. The demolition work moved along the terrace towards it and then stopped three houses short. It started up again a few empty streets away and is now moving towards us from a different direction.

The painting has been defaced along its lower edge. Above this, the same distorted faces continue to stare down at us. The mural is of a market scene with two lines of stalls receding to a horizon midway up the wall. A great deal of symmetry has been imposed, but the overall effect is ruined by a lack of perspective and by the careless contributions of the youths. They have no sense of depth or of light and shade and the faces they have painted are too uniformly coloured.

On either side of the wall, two wooden buttresses have been erected to protect and support it. These add to the illusion of security. Bottles are smashed against the scene but do little damage. Articles have appeared in local newspapers. There are even post-cards of the mural in some of the few remaining local shops. Farouk has bought several, but overall his collection continues to decline. It is not what his relatives back home in the desert would want to see.

In the bottom right-hand corner of the mural is a man with an elongated white face. He is wearing a shapeless overcoat and stands with his hands against his cheeks. He is well enough painted to have been done by the artist himself. His mouth is open and his tongue and teeth are visible. He has blue eyes and brown hair. In the entire scene he is the only figure looking out on to the street, the only one making any statement about the function of the mural and what is happening around it. He is the only one who betrays the painting's sense of containment, its exact and calculated design. Unlike most of the other figures, he has not yet been identified.

Along the terrace other families continue to leave. They are no more 'families' than we are, but this is how they think of themselves and what, ultimately, makes their dispersal so tragic. We watch them go and wish they would depart less conspicuously. Some of them have filled hired vans with pieces of furniture and rolls of carpet. Others move out with rucksacks and carrier bags. The vans run the length of the street with their horns blaring. The people with carrier bags go without pausing or looking back.

A neighbour spent a week carefully removing the stained-glass fanlight from above his door. On the morning of his departure the delicate frame was knocked over and smashed. He wept when he saw what had happened and then broke each of the small panes which had survived the accident. Few of those leaving take everything they possess with them, and although what is left is worthless, the rooms remain semi-furnished until either the vagrants or wreckers move in.

In one instance, the landlord went first and the remaining tenants completely demolished his room within an hour of his departure.

On several occasions, gangs of youths have gathered to ransack the more recently abandoned homes, taking out handfuls of crockery to smash in the road. One departee left a forwarding address pinned to his door.

Piles of rubbish and broken furniture line the street. A large maroon-coloured carpet has been salvaged by some of the vagrants and spread over the waste land beside their fires. They sprawl on it during the day like Turkish sultans with bottles instead of grapes. They have become increasingly defiant of the people around them and no longer abandon the empty houses before the arrival of the demolition crews. Several have exposed themselves to passing women and most piss openly in the gutter.

If the tramps spoke to me I ignored them. I ignored everyone I did not know.

Several days later a bulldozer arrived and cleared the road of rubble, once again allowing access to the sparse traffic.

Mrs D complained to us about the tramps. She said that living on the ground floor left her exposed to their 'advances'. The Irishman began to spend days alone with her in her room. He worked less often, but did not appear unhappy at his enforced idleness. Whenever Mrs D wanted to go out she intercepted one of us in the hallway and we walked along the street with her. We allowed her to slide her arm into ours. Farouk even began to make a point of calling for her as he set off into the city each day. He was still the most smartly dressed of us all and she always accepted his offer. I seldom went out until the evening and was always home before her.

The Irishman sat alone where the edge of the rubble met the pavement and spread out on to the road. He sat on what, a day previously, had been the doorstep of the Clover Leaf Bar. There had been a party a fortnight earlier to celebrate the closing night. The bar had been emptied of drink. Dust and tatters of paper still blew around the site. He sat with his head low and his arm wrapped around his knees. Hearing me approach he slapped a hand to the bottle protruding from his pocket. Seeing me, he relaxed. I sat beside him.

'It's come to something,' he said, pointing over his shoulder. A woman with a pram stopped and stared at us. I stared back and drove her away. 'We saw some good nights,' he went on absently. 'Some good nights.' He took the bottle from his pocket, drank from it and passed it to me. Across the road a gang of workmen were removing slabs of terracotta decoration from around the door of a small chapel.

'Will they save it, do you think?'

'I doubt it – not if they're already salvaging pieces.' Several churches had already been razed.

The Irishman stood up, stretched, and sat down again. Behind us a flock of gulls rose from the rubble. Seeing them surprised me.

'Come in off the river,' he explained. 'The docks.'

I asked him if he'd made any arrangements for his departure.

'Now there's a question,' he said. It was what he always said to avoid answering. 'Let's just say I've done as much as anyone else, yourself included.' He winked at me and drank again from the bottle, holding it between his knees as he rolled and lit a cigarette.

'The Barrel and the Duke of York went the week before,' he said. 'We're being driven out.' He let the smoke run over his face and coughed violently. It was the cough I'd heard in the depths of the night in the silent house. When he'd finished he took several deep breaths and spat on to the road. After that we sat in silence. There was frost on the ground and the cold penetrated my shoes and coat. Across the road the workmen began using heavy hammers to smash away the brickwork around the chapel porch.

'And what about the graveyard?' he said unexpectedly. 'What about the poor dead souls in there?'

I wondered how drunk he was.

'The graveyard?'

'The resting place of blessed Mrs D's blessed worn-out husbands.'

I told him I didn't know and then made a few obvious guesses as to what would happen.

'And they'll dig up all those poor blessed boxes and burn the buggers, and spread out their stones on the pavement of a shopping mall somewhere for the shoppers to walk on.'

I said he was probably right.

'And do you think she cares?'

'Mrs D?'

'Who else? I tell you –' he hesitated and looked around us before going on. 'I tell you, she cares no more for them two poor dead souls than she does for any one of us still living.'

I told him that she always gave me the impression of being very fond of them.

He shook his head. 'She protects herself with her memories of them, that's all she does. Who can blame her? What's she ever had since?' He unscrewed the cap from the bottle. '*Us* – that's all she's ever had since.' His fondness for Mrs D returned, and before drinking he raised the bottle to her. I wondered if he and she had made any arrangements to go on seeing each other after our dispersal.

A group of small children ran into the road and stood watching us. One of them carried a salvaged curtain rail with a pair of heavy curtains still attached. Another held a long length of washing line, tied to which was a small dog. The Irishman looked up and told them to piss off. They shouted abuse at us. It occurred to me that they had mistaken us for vagrants. They threw stones and the Irishman leapt to his feet and growled. They took fright and ran. The Irishman began to walk away, and by the time I caught up with him he was holding a conversation with himself.

'Do you think she knows about the graves?' I asked.

'Neither knows nor cares. She never even went to visit them nor to cut back the bit of grass or lay a few blooms.' He stopped and shook his head.

'She has the maisonette,' I said, being able to think of nothing else to say.

'Ah, yes, she has her maisonette. She has her nice new little house somewhere.'

We continued walking towards home. It was mid-afternoon and would soon be dark. In the distance we heard the sound of the demolition work.

'Knock 'em over, knock 'em down, bring me their heads for half a crown.' He stopped, smiling to himself at the memory it evoked. In the windows of some of the inhabited houses there were already fairy lights and small artificial Christmas trees and triangles of white spray in the corner of the panes. The few people we passed avoided looking at us.

He stopped me with a hand on my arm. 'Is it because of this –?' He waved the bottle. 'Is it because you think I'm an alcoholic?'

I said I didn't understand.

'They all think it. They all –' He stopped, released my arm and apologized. 'It used to be drunkard,' he said. 'And then all the drunkards became alcoholics. One minute we were there and the next we'd all disappeared. They – I –' He almost fell over a beam of wood which lay across the pavement. He prevented himself from falling but lost his grip on the bottle, which smashed and spread its contents invisibly over the wet ground. At the end of our terrace he stopped and buttoned up his overcoat, pushing the hair from his eyes and smoothing it flat.

'We'll have a get-together come Christmas,' he said. 'You, me, the darkies. Her idea.' The prospect appealed to me no more then than it had done when Mrs D had first suggested it. We waited to cross the road and he swore at the passing traffic. The puddles were already rimmed with ice and the passing cars shot up a fine spray.

The door was open and in the hallway he waited until I'd begun to climb the stairs before indicating that he intended calling on Mrs D. I stood on the landing and watched him fade into the shadow of the corridor leading to her room. He knocked and a strip of pale light spread the length of the hallway. I heard him say something and her laugh. The light narrowed and disappeared. I wondered if what he'd said about her husbands had been true, or if it had been an excuse for something else.

I always expected my room to be warm after the bitter cold of the stairs, but it never was.

I have seen Lynette twice since my departure: once at her mother's funeral, and again, years later, in the city centre, with another man.

I was alerted to the news of her mother's death by a newspaper headline. The idea of her having died pleased and reassured me. 'Dog Woman's Victory Marred by Personal Tragedy.' The article explained how Lynette had competed in a national dog show only hours after hearing that her mother had died. There were no details relating to the circumstances of the death. Lynette took two firsts and a second place. It was probably a painless and timely death, but I found myself wishing it otherwise. I liked also the idea of the newspaper referring to Lynette as 'Dog Woman'. I repeated the two words over and over until they no longer made any sense. I noted the time and place of the funeral and attended it.

It rained. Lynette stood among, but slightly apart from, her mother's sisters, refusing to be comforted by them. The vicar intoned over the open grave and the men of the family stood in a group beside another family plot.

I positioned myself some way behind them, sheltering in the lee of a marble angel whose outstretched wings protected me completely. Most of the women dabbed at their faces and watched Lynette. She stood closest of all to the open grave and those around her shared uneasy glances, as though they believed she might make a sudden, dramatic gesture and spoil the occasion. Several of the younger men had loosened their ties, and before the service they had held cigarettes in their cupped hands and waved the smoke away from their faces.

During the service someone noticed me and several of them turned. The vicar threw a sod of wet soil into the grave. Someone told Lynette I was present, and she too finally turned round. I raised my hand. She looked at me and looked away. Everyone else went on staring. I had arrived deliberately to ruin their occasion.

As those around the grave moved away from it I walked towards Lynette. The others, uncertain how to respond, cleared a path for me. She asked me what I wanted. I told her I'd seen the piece in the newspaper. 'I suppose you're happy now,' she said, indicating the grave. I said I was sorry. She said 'I'll bet', and walked past me. I shouted after her. The uncut grass soaked my shoes and trousers. I grabbed her arm but was unable to turn her to face me. She shook herself free and waited for the other women to join her. One of them asked me if I didn't think I'd done enough. My arguments were defeated by their hostile looks. Lynette refused even to look at me. Some of the men came forward. Several of the younger ones nodded in recognition and one of them called me 'pal' and told me not to cause any trouble.

I asked Lynette again if we could talk. She said we had nothing to talk about. I told her I'd made the effort to come to the funeral. The vicar interrupted us, said he understood, and succeeded in making the women around us angry by his inclusion of me in the proceedings.

I asked Lynette if I could contact her.

'Why?'

I had no answer. We had been apart for five years.

'As far as I'm concerned –' she began. The women around her listened avidly.

'I'll give you my address,' I said.

'Send it.' She moved away and the women followed her, just as the dogs had done. The men parted around me.

I walked back to the shelter of the marble angel and watched them leave. They filled a line of waiting cars and drove away. The vicar returned, walking with his head bowed as though looking for something he'd lost in the grass. He didn't see me and I did nothing to attract his attention. When he'd gone I moved to the open grave and looked down at the coffin. The rain was falling on it and the clods of earth remained unbroken on the lid.

My second sighting of Lynette took place in the city centre

several years later. It was late autumn, but bright and warm enough for me to be out on one of my aimless walks. I was about to emerge from a side street when Lynette walked across my path only a few feet ahead of me. If she'd turned or even glanced to one side she could not have avoided seeing me. I froze and looked away, and when she'd passed I moved out into the street and followed her. It was then that I saw she was holding the arm of a man, and that he was much taller and more heavily built than myself. They were talking, and occasionally she laughed. It sounded strange until I realized how seldom I had heard it before. I waited behind them at a controlled crossing, moving close enough to touch her.

I followed them into a large store. She was buying clothes and the man sat on a seat outside the changing rooms, looking impatient and embarrassed. She emerged and showed him what she had chosen. He approved of everything. Even these simple exchanges seemed to expose an intimacy we had never shared. I tried to imagine what kind of man he was. She had lost weight and seemed younger. She had made an effort with her appearance and her hair was styled differently.

They left the store arm in arm and went into a bar. The man greeted everyone already there and they responded noisily to his arrival. Lynette moved in his wake, sitting beside him in seats that were vacated for them. She looked suddenly out of place, as though it was the first time she'd been there. The man had only to raise his hand for more drinks to be delivered to them. As people entered the bar they saw him and made a point of speaking to him. Lynette was neglected and I watched her go through the uncomfortable motions of trying to appear involved and interested.

They remained in the bar until the middle of the afternoon. When they came out the long evening had almost begun. The man signalled for a taxi. On his wrist he wore gold bracelets, which slid up and down his arm. A taxi drew up and they climbed in.

When I arrived home, it was dusk. Where the demolition work had recently begun there were no lights, and the glowing city centre seemed to be almost completely ringed with darkness, like a burning island behind me.

I have not seen her since. It is my last memory of her.

The local cinema had been the first of our landmarks to go. With its blue and pink pitted stucco front it had always looked to me more like a Mexican church in a B movie Western than the Palace of Varieties it had once been. Half demolished, it became the most attractive of our ruins. It went finally at the height of summer, and for a month beforehand showed free matinées of all the films it still possessed.

I went once with the Patels, twice with Farouk, and fourteen times with Mrs D. The films were unremarkable and of poor quality, and were frequently interrupted by the noise of the workmen removing the fittings. Occasionally, a few of the vagrants found their way in. Most slept, but a few stayed awake to abuse the leading ladies and shout like children at whoever or whatever threatened them. A historical preservation society had tried to save the cinema, but to no avail.

Mrs D ate chocolates and told me of the films she'd seen with her husbands. When we emerged into the afternoon sunlight she wanted to walk rather than return to the house. We were beginning to detach ourselves from it even then.

I asked her if she'd seen *The Alamo* and pointed out the similarities.

She said 'Kirk Douglas', and absently pressed a dimple into her chin.

On the day the dust finally settled on the cinema and her reminiscences there were children in the street with rolls of unwound film. She retrieved an empty can and kept it as a souvenir.

All this was at a time before Farouk started his job at the club, when he was still working temporarily as a walking advertisement board for a promotions firm, coming home dressed as a hamburger or teapot, embarrassing us all and followed by a line of shouting children and barking dogs. He'd arrived home once as an Edam cheese with a wedge missing, from which he grinned whitely and distributed leaflets. We had to dismantle him before he could get through the front door. The red- and cream-coloured pieces of cheese remained in the hallway. Mrs D said she'd always wanted to go to Holland. 'To see the bulbs.' She closed her eyes and hummed 'Tulips from Amsterdam'.

For his final promotion Farouk had arrived home as a giant, three-coloured ice-cream cone, having walked the streets proclaiming the opening of a Neapolitan ice-cream parlolur in the West End. It was hot and the ice cream made him sweat. The proprietor of the parlour had wanted an Italian. Farouk came closest. He said the work was demeaning and that he was sick of posing with American tourists for photographs. I said the situation could have been much worse, but when he asked me how I couldn't think of an answer. At the height of the summer he'd worn the cheese and teapot and ice-cream cornet with only his shorts, shoes and socks underneath. No one would let him on a bus and it took him over an hour to walk to work, after which he walked for another eight.

I'd been with Farouk to see *The Sound of Music* twice, and on both occasions he'd cried. He said it was uplifting to see how other people responded to adversity. Julie Andrews usurped Doris Day as his favourite actress.

With the Patels I'd seen *Bhowani Junction* starring Stewart Granger and Ava Gardner. Mrs Patel had shouted her criticisms throughout the film and foreign voices had answered her back from the gloom. Mr Patel tried to appear as though he were not with us. She shouted at the slightest excuse, and there were times when she seemed almost to be providing a running commentary for the voices in the dark. Her husband said she had always been public spirited and tried to cover his ears.

At the end of the film Mrs Patel stood up and applauded. Mr Patel said we should never have come and tried to usher her out. We stood outside in the vivid light and heat and rubbed our eyes. Mrs Patel re-enacted several of Ava Gardner's scenes and her husband stiffened with embarrassment. She wanted to go again, but he said he could not afford to spend any more time away from the shop.

On the way home we'd encountered Farouk as a walking hamburger. He walked in the gutter beside us, constantly wiping the sweat from his face and flicking it to the ground.

Mrs D had seen Ava Gardner in *Two Girls and a Sailor* and *Mogambo*.

Farouk was unable to turn his head. He waited for her to finish before asking to be dismantled. Mrs D said something obvious about him bringing his work home with him and laughed. I heard only her second husband. Farouk ran a cold bath and sat in it for an hour. He swore every evening to resign, but set out each morning oozing sauce and mustard and thinking only of the money. He said that without the job he would have had no self-respect. He rose from the teapot, its lid a wide sombrero on his head. There was just room inside for him to move his arms, and a slot in the spout through which he distributed leaflets.

Mrs Patel returned alone to the free matinées and watched them without understanding a word of what was being said. She saw *The Cruel Sea* and made an explosion with her hands. She saw *Mrs Minniver* and whistled like a falling bomb.

The destruction of the cinema was our first real loss, the first realization that we were to be deprived of considerably more than our familiar surroundings.

Farouk drew the line at a walking pizza and shortly afterwards found his job at the club. Summer ended with a thunderstorm and even the coloured stucco of the cinema front was crushed and buried in the spreading rubble.

In the weeks before Christmas several new tenants arrived, stayed a few days, a week, a fortnight at the most, and then went. They occupied the vacant rooms on the third and fourth floors and spent as little time as possible in the house. They kept themselves apart from us and on the few occasions we passed them on the stairs we, in turn, ignored them. They were tenants from the houses already demolished and they all had somewhere else to go. Because of this we resented their presence. Mrs D rejoiced at the money they brought in. They expected nothing from her in return. For them the house had simply become an address, vital for the continued payment of whatever the state was paying them.

A family arrived. The children fought with the Patel children. At night the Irishman came home drunk and shouted obscenities through their door, always apologizing when he saw them the following day. The woman had tight black hair and a face so heavily freckled that it appeared almost red. She spent most of their short stay cooking large meals, filling the house with the unfamiliar smell of roasting meat.

Two much older women arrived. They said they were sisters and that they had both been famous dancers in their day. They showed everyone photographs of themselves that had been taken at least half a century ago. Mrs D argued with them over the payment of their rent. They demanded that she leave their room and then slammed the door behind her.

There was a fire in a neighbouring empty house. We stood in the street and watched it burn. The fire brigade arrived and put it out.

The water from the hoses filled the road and the garden of the house was piled with charred wood.

Last night I saw Farouk at work. He stood in the doorway of a club in a street lined with clubs, at the entrances to which stood other men, each of them wearing the same colourful jacket of which he was so proud. Above them, suspended in the darkness, hung a tangle of flickering neon. There were also illuminated displays around the doorways: women cupping their breasts, or standing with their legs apart, their hands on their hips. Above Farouk's doorway was a line of coloured bulbs which flashed down at him.

I watched him from the entrance to an alley on the opposite side of the street, careful that he should not see me.

I had come across him entirely by accident.

Groups of men moved along the street, studying the displays until the doormen led them inside, congratulating them on their choice. They held their hands firmly against the men's backs. If they worked on a commission basis, then the success of one was only too obviously the failure of the others.

Farouk's job, the job about which we had all been told so much, and of which he was so proud, was to stand in a doorway, open the door and hold it open.

I watched him for an hour, and because no one either entered or left he had nothing to do. This was his 'Great Fortune'. He talked with the other men, but only when spoken to. He seemed happier to be left alone, coming out of his doorway less often than the others, preferring to remain in the patch of shadow beneath the flashing lights. It was cold and all the men stamped their feet and blew into their cupped hands. Farouk wore a burgundy velvet jacket with contrasting lapels, and burgundy trousers with a silver stripe down each leg. Under the jacket he wore a white shirt and bow tie. He looked like an entertainer and continually straightened his collar and picked dust from his shoulders and sleeves. When someone appeared who looked as though they might go into his club, he stood to attention and smiled at them, moving out of the shadow and into the glare of the neon lights.

He looked unhappy and out of place and I had the impression that he would pretend not to recognize me if I passed in front of him. I wondered how important to him his job of opening and holding doors really was.

As I watched, a younger man, another Arab, appeared in the doorway beside him. The man looked each way along the street and called for the attention of those in the nearest doorways. Then he held Farouk's cheeks in both hands, whispered something and squeezed his face. I guessed from Farouk's reaction that the man was the owner of the club, his benevolent employer. The other men either laughed or cheered. The man released Farouk, stepped into the street and bowed. Then he positioned himself behind Farouk, pressed himself close and began to make suggestive movements. Farouk was forced to bend his knees and move with him. Along the street the cheering grew louder. Even when prospective customers appeared, the club owner continued with what was quite obviously a familiar routine. For Farouk's sake I hoped it all meant something quite different to him. When the man had finished he crossed the street to inspect the tall narrow front of the building in which his club was housed. I looked up and saw a woman sitting in an upper-storey window. She waved down to him. The man blew her a kiss. Then he beckoned Farouk from his shadow into the middle of the street and repeated with him the same degrading routine for her benefit. This time when they had finished Farouk pulled away. The man reacted angrily, jabbing his finger into Farouk's face, forcing it into his cheek. Then he returned indoors, leaving Farouk alone at the centre of the street.

Farouk took out a handkerchief and wiped his face, folded it neatly into a triangle and wedged it back into his breast pocket.

I left him, wondering how I would react to his lies when I saw him the following day.

The ground was to open up and swallow the house, then to close over it and leave nothing. The dust would settle and the house and its inhabitants would no longer exist. People from outside would be invited to inspect the site and make guesses as to what had happened there. Schoolchildren would be led over it on rambles. Only an echo of its destruction would remain, a final dislodged brick settling, a cacophony of the sounds of which the house had once been composed. The noise would be compressed into bursts of only a few seconds, drawing to a close with Mrs Patel's wailing, and culminating in the final, abrupt scream of the mutilated body. Cracks would appear in the brickwork which corresponded with the wounds opening in the skin. We would all be aware of what was happening, but would be too involved in what we were doing to save ourselves. We would stand mesmerized, formed into a tight circle around the flailing arms and kicking legs. The body would move like a crawling baby tipped on to its back. Only the insignificant details would have changed. Pipes and cables would be severed, the vital organs of our existence placed under too great a stress.

My back is cold, my face warm. The ground beneath me opens yet my feet remain firmly together. Lynette arrives to watch our destruction. She scatters silver coins over us and as the dust begins to settle she is the first to move through it, wiping it from her expensive clothes. I am above her, looking down. I am beneath her, crushed to nothing.

Two strangers arrive, men of similar ages, each looking for his wife. They each describe a different woman. Mrs D stands perfectly still in the shadow of her room until they have gone.

It has rained continually since the end of November. It is raining now. The meteorological experts have forecast a hard winter and have warned against its likely consequences continuing into the new year. This is as explicit as they are prepared to be. In the house we are indifferent to the news. Here, our concern at what is happening expresses itself in other ways. It has manifested itself, for instance, in cheap Christmas decorations in the hallway. Mrs D hung them on the first of December and we were all invited to comment on them. They were her gift to us all. She did not think she would be taking them with her to her new home.

Zigzagging along the dark corridor were spirals of crêpe paper and standing on the hall table was a small tree, already with a fall of silver needles around its base. It was decorated with glass balls and a string of lights which did not work. Seeing the tree made me wonder – for no apparent reason other than that the passage of time seemed recently to have accelerated – how long ago the date of our eviction had finally been decided upon. Plans to demolish the house may even have been in hand before my arrival.

We run the gauntlet of colour in the hallway each time we enter and leave – all, that is, except for Farouk, who has once again resorted to the fire escape. I warned him against it icing over and he replied that the risk was worthwhile.

Only Mr Patel and the Irishman seemed genuinely pleased at Mrs D's simple attempts at decoration. The Irishman told her she reminded him of his mother, simultaneously flattering and offending her. They are of a similar age, although there are nights when he appears much older. Mr Patel explained to her about celebrations in India, in which she made the effort to appear interested before drawing another compliment from him. Mrs Patel stood beside me and looked down at her husband in the hallway. She tutted and made faces at everything he said. The following day he arrived home with a carton of decorations with which their own room was rapidly over-festooned, and which both myself and the Irishman were invited in to admire. He offered us all a drink and we toasted his decorations. The two small children stood watching us and made us feel uneasy. Each child held a yellow balloon and had tinsel wrapped around its forehead. We drank a second toast to their health, and a third to Mrs Patel's unborn child.

By beginning our celebration of Christmas early, its significance and effect have been diluted. After a week most of the streamers had come down and the tree had been broken from its stand. The two West Indians treated it all as a joke and so were pointed out by Mrs D as being the perpetrators of the crime. Mr Patel said she was welcome to the surplus decorations from his own room, after which his wife shouted at him for an hour.

Farouk caught hold of my arm and nodded towards my door. I asked him what he wanted. He held his cocked head a few inches from the Patels' door, came back to me and whispered that he had found a flat, a good flat, a very good flat, a very very good flat. I congratulated him. A very very good flat that had to be shared with someone else. Before I could speak, he told me where it was and what it cost. I said I was sure he would find someone. He started to protest, sighed melodramatically, and said I was right. I asked him if he'd actually been to see it. He shook his head. I asked him when he intended going. He shrugged. Someone at the club had told him about the flat. It was a good place to work for picking up that kind of information. One way or another we were all beginning to disappoint each other.

He followed me from the landing into my room. Inside, he said I was lucky. I asked him why, but he couldn't explain. He sat at the table, toyed with his tie and medallion and looked like a child – like one of the children, in fact, who accompanied him up the fire escape into his room.

'I have made many friends,' he said absently, as though the line had been rehearsed for the benefit of someone who didn't know him.

I suggested that someone at the club might want to share with him. He still did not know that I had seen him in the doorway. He watched me closely as he answered. I offered him a cigarette and he accepted.

'Do you think the Patels might be interested to hear about the flat?' He told me again how good it was.

'The children . . .' I said.

'Ah, yes, the children.'

'You could mention it to muscle man, he might be interested.'

'You think so?'

'Certainly. Room for expansion.' My forced optimism convinced neither of us.

'It was just an idea,' he said. 'There are always plenty of flats. We will all find a new flat.'

I agreed with him, and wondered at the real cause of his concern. The noise from the Patels' rose above its usual level and we both turned to look.

'They argue,' he said.

I told him that I didn't think it was actually arguing.

He spoke about the club, but with little of his former enthusiasm. He said he was looking for a new job because things hadn't turned out as he'd expected them to. I told him it was a common problem.

He ran his palm over the papers scattered across the table and said he looked forward to reading whatever it was I was writing.

'Me too,' I said.

He misunderstood and assured me that I would be remembered long after I was dead. He invested this with a great deal of importance, as though he believed that he too would somehow share in my future good fortune.

I asked him how his family were and whether or not he was still sending them the slides. He said that an uncle had started sending back postcards of his home town, of expensive tourist hotels, swimming pools and casinos, of places that neither he nor the remainder of his family had ever visited or had even the remotest chance of visiting in the future. He said he could not understand why. Then he tapped his forehead and said that the uncle had always been considered strange, that he was from his mother's side and *they* had all been country-dwellers before coming to the town. The uncle, I realized, was playing him at his own game. When Farouk screwed a finger into his temple I did the same and nodded gravely. I asked him how long it had been since his last visit home. He counted out the years on both hands.

'Very little justice in the world,' he said, as though continuing a completely different conversation. 'Persecution, that's the word.'

'Are you being persecuted?'

'Me personally, no. Not me personally.'

'I see.' Silence followed. To break it I asked him again if he intended to go and see the flat.

'I have to go to work.'

'Will you go tomorrow?'

'If there is time.' He adopted the formal, impersonal tone with which he seemed more confident and relaxed.

The noise from the Patels' resumed.

'He is not at his shop today?'

'No.'

'She eats him up and spits him out.'

'Something like that. It works for them.'

'It would not suit everyone.'

'No, I suppose not.' His formality made me feel uncomfortable and I was relieved when he finally went.

'If you change your mind about the flat . . .' he said.

'I doubt it.'

He looked from my face to my chest. 'No, I suppose not.'

When he had gone I slipped the catch on the door. My hand was shaking, as though I had been in some way threatened.

There are no longer any lights in the windows of the opposite terrace and my rear window now looks out on to a continuous blank wall, its horizon broken only by the tangle of cables and aerials which remain. I cannot decide whether the houses have finally been abandoned or if their electricity has been disconnected. Either way, it is something else that has gone. Mrs D's unsolicited opinion is that the houses are empty. To hear her speak, they have become an enemy ship drawn alongside.

Seeing the emptiness at the rear as well as the devastation to the front, our own fate is assured. Mrs D still speaks of the 'nerve' of the powers behind what is happening. I ask her to leave and am immediately part of the conspiracy against her. There is talk of compensation. There has always been talk of compensation. The talk of compensation will continue long after we have gone. She wants to know how anyone can put a price on what she has been through. I ask her again to leave. I am sitting at the window, looking out. She accuses me of being morbid. We should have been decisive. We should have fought. None of this should ever have happened. She is the star of a thousand Ealing comedies. She remembers the war. 'The Blitz,' she said suddenly, cheered by the comparison. I told her London could take it. She accused me of being sarcastic and defeatist. She had played her part, just as we were all now playing ours. The sky was the colour of charcoal streaked with red. She heard aircraft and bombs and started talking about bravery in the face of overwhelming odds. You always heard the bombs coming, never knew what to expect. There were comparisons she could make. She sat on the bed and I resigned myself to her staying.

She said the Irishman remembered the war, *her* war. I, on the other hand, did not remember it and so could not now be expected to understand. 'Better days,' she said. I asked her how she expected things to get any worse. She rose and went to the front window. Two men were composing a new picture on one of the hoardings. A giant coach and smiling sun promised Mediterranean holidays. Old women spent their winters in Spain. We faced each other from opposite ends of the room. She asked me if I ever thought about dying. She did. Her husbands had been preoccupied with dying. I expected her to confess to having murdered them. I told her I wanted to work. She didn't believe me.

'Irish talks about dying,' she said.

'He's Irish. They all do it.' I felt a sudden great sympathy for him.

'We're of an age,' she said, the pronouncement making everything clear.

When she went I remained at the rear window. There were moving lights and shadows in the empty terrace. The roof line faded into the sky. In the alley the scribbles of sprayed graffiti shone like climbing roses in the darkness.

Lynette sat with the squashed black and cream face of a pekinese held between herself and the bowl of cereal on the table. She read from a magazine beside her. Occasionally the dog reached forward and lapped milk from her bowl. She tapped it on the head and told it to stop. The animal's face disgusted me. Milk dripped from the fur on its chin. Lynette pulled back its jowls to demonstrate something she was trying to achieve in breeding the dogs. I asked her if she was going to carry on eating the cereal after the dog had licked the bowl. She dropped the dog to the floor and said she wasn't going to have that particular argument again.

'It's scarcely hygienic,' I said.

'Hygienic! These dogs are the cleanest –'

'Licking from our plates.'

'Examined and inoculated.'

'If one of the things comes near my plate . . .'

She laughed her loud, exaggerated laugh. 'Things! Things!'

I told her to forget it.

'Don't worry.' She returned to her magazine. The dog sat at her feet, looking up at me.

Later, her mother arrived and the two women sat together. Her mother picked up the small dog. 'Oh, dear dear dear dear dear. How could anyone say anything nasty about such a pretty little –'

'Easy,' I said, and said something nasty. She had been getting at me rather than pacifying the dog. She went through the motions of being mortally offended, of never having been spoken to like that in her entire life before. I asked her if she was sure and left her. I passed Lynette on her way in. 'Your mother's just dropped the precious peke,' I said. 'I think it bit her.'

Her mother spent the rest of the morning in the kennels. It was what she was paid to do, but she always managed to do it as though she were doing us a favour. I pointed out the piles of shit which needed clearing up. I called them this because it offended her more than the small wet piles themselves. She collected them into a dustpan without looking, and afterwards poured boiling water over the stains. After that I went out.

When I returned Lynette sat alone with an ashtray full of half-smoked cigarettes.

'You lied,' she said without looking up.

'I lied,' I said. 'So what?'

'You really hurt her.'

'I really hurt her.'

She stubbed out another cigarette.

'I don't suppose it matters to you, does it?' she said, rising from the table.

I pretended to think about it. 'No, I don't suppose it does.'

I went upstairs and fell asleep. When I awoke it was dark and Lynette was asleep in another room. After that we slept in separate beds nine nights out of ten.

' "An assessment –" '

'Robbery!'

' "An assessment for purposes of compensation relating –" '

'Daylight robbery.' She might as well lie down and die and let them take the lot. The offer was an insult. They were lying, thieving cheats who thought only of themselves, and took advantage of people like her. Who did they think they were? Who did they think she was?

I pointed out to her the paragraph which indicated that the sum in question had been agreed by her a year previously.

It was still robbery, daylight and dishonest and . . .

I stopped listening and concentrated on the cups of tea on the café table between us.

' . . . turning in their graves . . .' If they knew what was happening to her.

'Who?'

Guess.

Who did I think?

I apologized.

We sat opposite the Town Hall. A waitress wiped the table and cleared away the used crockery. Mrs D stopped speaking until she'd gone.

'Robbery.' Momentum.

I told her again that she'd already agreed to the sum. She said it was nice to know who your friends were, who you could trust. I went back to my tea.

A few minutes later she confessed to having been again to inspect her new home. I asked her what it was like. She said she still hadn't been able to get in. It was new, unlived in, rings of dried polish on its second-floor windows and surrounded by construction work, sites on which identical blocks were being raised. I knew from the way she spoke that the visit had disappointed her. I realized afterwards that it had also been the reason behind our useless visit to the Town Hall. I hadn't even been in with her. She referred to me as her 'moral support'. The waitress returned to our table with the bill. I asked Mrs D what she'd expected. Too much. Obviously. We were all in the same boat.

Mrs D has started accompanying the Irishman on his lunchtime drinking sessions. They return half drunk in the middle of the afternoon and sit together in her room. He listens to stories about her husbands and in turn tells her about the wife he abandoned in Ireland ten years ago. I cannot remember how I found out about his wife, but it has become an established fact in the house – one of the countless details, half truths and suppositions of which we are all composed in the eyes of the others. He talks about his wife as though she were a distant aunt, remembered from childhood. He also talks of her with affection, as though the decision to abandon her had been forced upon him against his will. She was a sick woman and he left her with several children. The number varies depending on why the rumour is being recycled, and by whom. Because they are both drunk, they talk loudly and their conversation rises through the ceiling into my room. I sit on my bed and listen. He is telling her about his misfortunes, and thus prompted she retaliates with her own. They are both comforted. The talk turns to money and she falls silent. She tells him that neither of her husbands would have approved. Their voices fade to a murmur and they are interrupted by the early return of Mr Patel. It is still only mid-afternoon and he is six hours early.

Following a brief argument with his wife, he knocked on my

door and I shouted for him to come in. He apologized for interrupting me. He heard the voices beneath us and paused to listen. Composing himself, he stood at the centre of the room, looking like a schoolboy about to be punished. I asked him why he'd returned so early.

'Ah, so you see . . .' He held out his hands to me.

'Are you taking a holiday?' It was a joke made at his expense, but he was too polite not to smile.

'The truth of the fact is that there is unforeseen trouble.'

'At the shop?'

'Spot on. Yes. Unforeseen.'

'With your brother-in-law, you mean?'

He sat at the table opposite me. 'He is a stubborn and calculating man. He has seen a legal aid and says I cannot force him to leave simply to use the flat for my own purposes.' He took out an envelope and passed it to me. It contained nothing more than a xeroxed fact sheet from a local law centre. Learning of our rights as tenants has been a succession of growing disappointments.

'Does he have a solicitor?' I asked.

'Why a solicitor?'

'You can forcibly evict him. Do you have any kind of agreement with him, written documents on the terms of his lease?' Hearing myself speak depressed me.

'No, nothing signed between us.'

'Then why not make it clear to him that you want him out because of his stealing?'

He sighed and looked at me as though he knew the fight was already lost. 'She will be upset.' He nodded in the direction of his room. 'I cannot afford to upset her, not with the child.'

'And does her own sister not care what happens to her, to the child?'

'She is a kind woman. She has given us clothes.'

'But not kind enough to let you move into the flat which is rightfully yours.'

'It is not her fault.' He folded the sheet of paper back into the envelope. Below us the voices rose, the Irishman's subsiding in a familiar bout of coughing.

'He sounds sick.'

'Drunk.'

'Ah, yes.'

I wanted to tell him to stop thinking of other people and to evict his brother-in-law. Instead, I asked him if he had the money to find a new flat. He said he had, but that neither the flat nor the money was the real problem. His brother-in-law's family were his only relatives in this country. And now, through what he considered to be his own inconsiderate actions, he had alienated them and was alone. I reminded him that he had his wife and children, but this served only to depress him even further.

'My advice is to go to the same law centre and seek advice on where you stand. They'll let you know what he can and can't do.'

'He will still be my brother-in-law.' His determination ended there. The man who had stolen from him and who was now depriving him of a home and security was the husband of the sister of the woman who carried his child. He could not even begin to look seriously for a fair solution to the problem.

'Had you decided all this before coming to see me?' I asked.

He nodded contritely. 'You are a friend,' he said. 'Your opinion . . .'

I told him there was no need to explain.

Below us the Irishman resumed his coughing. Mrs D was singing. Mr Patel said she was a woman with spirits, and when I told him that he'd made a joke he laughed and said that his customers always considered him a very amusing man.

The anniversary of her second husband. All in all not the man the first had been. Ten years married, and then dead. I'd known her for almost as long as he had. The second husband had been no gardener, had tried for her sake, but had failed. In ten years there was not a skirting board painted, a leaking tap fixed or a squeaking hinge oiled. A year on his deathbed, looking back (and talking about, always talking about) the useless sixty which had gone before. He'd been fifteen years older than her when they'd married, something she was at pains to point out. As his life came to a close he appeared to have seen a lot of loose ends and had chosen his deathbed as the place from which to draw them together. It was a miracle that he did not have access to pen and paper or his thoughts would be with us still, undiluted by her own. She remembers him fondly, another tear in her eye, not wanting to show or be accused of preferential treatment. Today *his* photograph has been taken down and dusted, and that of the other turned to the wall.

A small man with oiled hair, and always in his shirt sleeves as though he were about to attend to any one of the thousand or so small jobs which went neglected during his time in the house. His trick seems to have been to make himself appear as though he were always *about* to do something useful. A drinker, like the other, but one who indulged in the ritual of preparing himself, of cleaning, trimming, dressing, brushing and presenting himself for inspection and praise. A man who had known how to have a good time. It was what she missed the most about him. Now all that was left of him was another small celebration, a month after the first, and a month before the shrine to both of their memories finally succumbed to the nudge of the swinging lead weight and the gentle shove of the bulldozer.

Dead. Never to be replaced.

She'd cemented over the small front garden as a symbolic reburial of her first husband upon marrying the second, who complained of suffering from hayfever. He complained, it seemed, about a great deal. He never saw the point of rushing around and wearing himself out (another memory, another smile). He held claim to being the first man to declare that he was better off drawing unemployment benefit than working. 'Earnings related, then,' she said, half excusing him, half convincing us that he'd been right. He'd had an opinion on everything and they lingered still in her (his legacy). 'Chalk and cheese,' she said, 'the first and the second.' As a young man he'd been at Dunkirk, left his health in the sand, never been a fit man since. Lost it in service of King and –

Country?

Enough. A glare.

He'd been fit apart from his bad health, thoughtful apart from his loud-mouthed thoughtlessness, and had thought the world of her, despite having used her and lived off her. That kind of man – the kind it was better to look back fondly upon than to have present. She had been his third wife (another of his achievements).

It had been his idea for her to take in lodgers. Friends of his had done the conversion, put in the plumbing, re-wired the rooms (another of his legacies). Even the Irishman found it difficult to say anything nice about him. He existed now only as an excuse for remembering and for tears – a celebration of sorts.

She described him for us, but frequently paused to correct herself and disentangle him from her memories of Number One. He'd been well respected and had had many friends. His sick-bed was the bed in which she now slept. (He'd died in another – presumably one of the other beds in the house. No one asked which.) He'd been sixty-three and strong as an ox when he'd finally succumbed. (I suspect she even confused him with her mother, who had similarly confounded the doctors and had been as unfairly felled.) She made him sound like a man who had been unjustly punished, and who might be alive yet but for his disbelieving accusers. But the loss had been his alone and, as with most losses, she made considerably more of it than it warranted. The baton of suffering had been handed on to her.

Tight brown curly hair he'd had, and always smiling, always ready with a joke or good word. Bit of a ladies' man. But never went too far. Knew when to stop. Always civil and courteous. Always ready to listen. I began to wonder if he hadn't after all made a list of his virtues and left them to her in lieu of anything more substantial.

Farouk said to me afterwards that the man reminded him of his uncle. If we'd been outside he would have spat on the ground.

She, of course, wouldn't hear a harsh word said against him.

Mr Patel asked her what his profession had been.

'Entrepreneur' was the term he'd always preferred. She liked the word, it conferred a kind of status.

I resented the domination of Number Two over Number One, of the way he'd tried to make himself appear resourceful and interesting. I wondered how much of what she said she really believed, and how much of it was simply a form of protective momentum, past versus present.

When at last she'd finished, she invited the Irishman and myself into her room for a drink. We accepted unwillingly and went with her to worship at the shrine of the curly-haired, smiling man (neither attribute being much in evidence in the photograph itself), and drank to his – she almost said good health, but it seemed the least appropriate of his many qualities to celebrate. Ten happy years was the eventual choice. The Irishman drank five glasses of two years each, each refill raised in homage. It made her happy to see it. It was what (as always) he would have wanted. He'd never read a book and yet even I would have found it hard not to like him. He'd hated the Irish, and yet . . . The Irishman said he understood and felt entitled to pour himself another drink.

The one thing her husband would not have had in the house were the – eyes raised, a finger pointing upwards, a word mouthed.

'Xenophobia,' I said, unable to resist.

'Towards the end,' she said. 'You name it, he had it.'

After an hour she said she wanted to be alone. As we got up to go she said tearfully that she'd promised him never to marry again. I told her we understood and we left her with whatever it was she still had of him.

Yesterday, Sunday, we were woken to the noise of a band. We stood at our windows and looked out. Down the centre of the deserted street marched squares of colourfully dressed children, flanked by adults in ones and twos. There were scouts, guides, Sunday-school groups and, at the head of the procession, a band of majorettes preceded by three baton-twirling girls who moved across the street at random, spinning their silver canes high into the air. At regular intervals the marchers turned and saluted the empty houses.

There followed several other, smaller bands, no two of them playing the same tune. There was no one on the street to watch the parade and I was convinced that either a wrong turning had been made or the organizers were unaware of what had taken place in the year since the last procession.

It was eight-thirty and two landings above me I heard the Irishman swearing loudly. The younger marching children appeared intimidated by the street's emptiness. Someone pointed out the watching vagrants and the still smouldering fires. The adults too seemed uncertain of their reasons for continuing.

In the house our responses were predictable. The Irishman continued to swear. Mrs D stood in the open doorway, half-raising her hand to each passing band. Mr and Mrs Patel stood outside my door and looked down through the landing window. Mrs Patel's excitement rose to a pitch at the sight of the elaborate banner into which a likeness of the Queen had been woven in pink and gold. I imagined it likely that Mr Patel would consider it his duty to salute the portrait.

I watched the entire parade from my window, wrapped in an eiderdown. At the end of the procession marched a few stragglers, parents and churchgoers, and behind them came Farouk, on his way home from the club, marching stiffly and swinging his arms. When those ahead of him saluted, so did he. He stopped outside the house and the parade moved on.

The open door filled the house with cold air. At the end of the street the marchers turned right and then right again, doubling back on themselves around the empty space opposite us. Watching them, I was more convinced than ever that they had made a mistake in their route. They were reduced now to strips of colour and their sound came back to us in snatches, like the music of a spun radio dial. The batons above the leaders caught the early sun and appeared as circles of light.

Three tremors hit the house, each one more powerful than the last. Dust settled on us from the ceiling. At the first shock the pictures on the wall shifted out of line, at the second they swung, and at the third they fell. Mrs Patel screamed. The West Indians ran to the door and threw it open. A beam of brilliant light flooded the room, solid with dust. A group of yellow-helmeted men looked in at us and shouted for us to leave. When we refused they gave up on us and walked away. Mrs D began replacing the pictures. The houses around us were being destroyed. We stood in the doorway to watch as walls fell in prearranged sequences, collapsing inwards and laying whole in slabs. Only Mrs Patel seemed excited at the spectacle. Her husband pointed out that it was shortly to happen to us. Mrs D shouted for someone to tell her if the pictures were straight. There was blood on her blouse, and on her hands and face where she had wiped her eyes and mouth. We were all coated in the fine powder and stood like statues. The Negro and his girl drew lines on each other's cheeks. Mrs D called them savages. They laughed at her. Atlas replaced the furniture which had shifted and fallen. Mr Patel brushed the powder of dust from his wife's hair. She closed her eyes and began to sing to him. I wanted to leave. Mrs D took the knife from me and said she understood. It faded and then disappeared in her hands. Atlas said we expected too much and were bound to be disappointed. He then went through the routine of flexing his muscles, beginning with his calves and working up to his neck. When he was certain that nothing had been damaged he performed for us, stripping down to his black trunks. I wanted to make him stop, to remind him – remind them all – of the purpose of our gathering. The sound of collapsing walls still reached us from outside and the beam of powerful light still dissolved everything it touched.

I left them and returned to my room. It too had been shaken by the tremors. My shelves of carefully arranged books lay at an untidy angle. One lay on the floor with its spine broken. From outside came the notes of what sounded like an accordion being badly played. It went on until I could stand it no longer and shouted for it to stop. It did, but started up again shortly afterwards. The harsh, discordant notes sounded like the racket of fighting birds. It ended finally with a prolonged wheeze, as though the instrument had been stood on its end and allowed to collapse under its own weight.

A month after my visit to look at the room above the Chinese take-away I watched as a hearse drew up and as two men wearing dark suits and gloves stood in the street outside. A column of Chinese emerged, the leaders carrying a coffin. The man and young woman followed them. The woman was sobbing convulsively and the man stood with his hands on her shoulders whispering to her. The others stood around them bowing with their hands together. A message composed of Chinese characters had been taped across the glass door of the shop. The man saw me but did not recognize me, and without a hat to remove there was no safe, anonymous gesture of respect I could make to either of them. Someone carried small bunches of flowers and ribbons from the shop and arranged them around the coffin. The card advertising the room was still in the window. The woman's crying rose and fell and filled the cold street.

Earlier in the week the man in the shabby suit had left the house. His arrival had caused more interest than his departure and, in his absence, we speculated on his hopeless circumstances, all of us careful not to say anything which might reflect on our own.

The following day two men carrying billiard-cue cases arrived. Mrs D mistook the cases for those of flutes. She asked the men if they were musicians, and they said they were. Afterwards, when I pointed out to her what the cases were for, she became offended. She said I knew nothing about billiards. I told her she knew nothing about flautists. The word threw her and she slammed the door on me.

The following day a small Indian woman arrived and read out her references. She asked for a room with a view, which at least suggested a sense of humour. Mrs D repeated the word 'references' as though it were a disease with which the woman might infect us all. Neither the woman nor the two men returned.

Yesterday, having arrived at the same conclusion reached by the rest of us months ago, Mrs D removed her card from the newsagent's window. She brought it back to the house with her and kept it alongside her husbands. Our boundaries are now self-regulating, capable of being breached only from within.

During the night the first full fall of snow of the year arrived. It covered the half-demolished buildings and piles of rubble and, for a morning at least, they might have been grassy knolls and picturesque ruins. On the road the snow turned quickly to water and the tramps built their fires higher and stayed with them all day. They were burning tyres and the smoke grew thicker and blacker and hung in a pall above the streets. A car was abandoned and they sat in it, drinking and making engine noises. By mid-morning most of the snow had gone. In places it froze, and icicles grew above both my windows.

The following morning there was no water in the pipes. The West Indians complained that the water was flooding from a tank above their room. Mrs D inspected the damage and invited me up to assess what needed to be done. I told her to call a plumber, and it only then became apparent that she expected *me* to solve the problem. Whatever repair was required, it needed only to be makeshift, to last a few weeks. The West Indians said they weren't satisfied. Mrs D said, 'Who cares?' She told them that the fault was partly theirs for having let the room get too cold. There were two bar heaters burning and the room was still cold. They laughed at her and said that if the pipe wasn't fixed then they were within their rights to withhold their rent. She laughed back at them and said, 'Rights! Rights!' They backed down. She looked at the posters on their walls and said they should thank me for offering to repair the damage they'd caused. Then she gave me five pounds for a waterproof bandage, taking the note from her purse as though it were her last.

When it melted the snow brought more water into my room. I had long since abandoned my requests for the leak to be fixed. In the mornings the windows were coated inside and out with ice, and in the permanent shadows the snow lasted for over a week.

Mrs Patel slipped on the pavement and sprained her ankle. Her husband asked if I would visit her during the day. I did. He said he had spent sleepless nights thinking about their unborn child. His wife played the helpless invalid to the hilt, sitting with her leg along the sofa and wincing with pain at the slightest movement or mention of it. I knew from what I saw in the flat around her that she could in fact move, and because she could not understand a word I said, I told her so. Her husband left notes thanking me for my kindness and generosity. When I saw him he said he was worried that the sprain wasn't healing as quickly as the doctor had said it would. He brought her chocolates and fruit from the shop. I told him not to worry.

It snowed again a few days later, and the Irishman stopped going out to work altogether. He said it was because of the weather. He went out for four hours every lunchtime and returned drunk, repeating the process in the evening. He showed me a wallet packed tight with ten-pound notes and said he doubted if he would continue in the construction trade for much longer. Then he laughed and shook my arm until I joined him. He said that he had plans and laughed again when I asked him what they were. He asked me if I didn't think Mrs D was a desirable woman. When I repeated his words to her, she said he reminded her of her first husband.

During the following week the weather worsened and there were sunless days when it seemed scarcely to get light between the late dawns and early evenings.

'The time is coming for us all to make a decision,' Mr Patel announced. It sounded like the opening of a prepared speech, which it probably was. Beside him, his wife nodded gravely, confirming that this dramatic opening had been long considered. Her sprained ankle had mended overnight and although she could have understood almost nothing of what her husband was saying, she continued to either shake or nod her head at everything he said. She had gained weight during the previous weeks but still did not look pregnant.

Mr Patel quoted something Winston Churchill had said about times of adversity. At the mention of the name the Negro turned and watched him suspiciously. His girlfriend stood beside him. Mrs

Patel clapped. She clapped again when her husband had finished. It was a fortnight till Christmas.

Mr Patel stepped back and waited for someone else to speak. I said I saw little reason why any of us should now come to a decision concerning our individual fates having remained indecisive for so long. Only Mr Patel took this calmly, saying in my defence that it was a weakness in us all. His wife, realizing I had spoken out against him, scowled at me.

'Who care what happen?' one of the West Indians said. 'Is nothing we any of us can do about it.' He waved the envelope addressed to the flat in which he lived. Mrs D agreed and then disagreed with him, waiting for someone else to take up the argument.

We had gathered together in Mrs D's downstairs room. That alone was something of an occasion. There wasn't one of us who didn't either suspect or mistrust the motives of at least half of the others. It was the first time Mrs Patel had been in the room and so, following her husband's opening speech, she spent more time inspecting its contents than actually listening to what was being said. The two West Indians shifted uncomfortably from foot to foot. The Negro shook his head at everything that was said and his girlfriend smiled at me. Mrs Patel nudged her husband at regular intervals and pointed at something with her little finger, the rest of her hand concealed in the folds of her sari. As usual, Mr Patel tried to agree with us all. We each held our own cups, which Mrs D had asked us to bring.

'I'll be moving on anyhow,' said the Irishman. His calm, off-hand manner surprised us and our collective inertia was once again exposed. I wanted to be brave enough casually to announce, 'Me, too.'

'When?' asked Mrs D. He said he didn't know. She watched him closely. 'You're perfectly at liberty, any of you, to leave when you choose,' she said. She then told those who didn't already know about the maisonette she had been offered. In our company, her relative good fortune made her nervous. Mrs Patel told us via her husband that they had received no such offer. Her husband explained to her that it was because they were only tenants, whereas Mrs D was the owner of the house. He then informed everyone of their plans to move into the flat above the shop. He signalled to me not to pursue the matter of his brother-in-law any further. His wife jabbed a finger into his stomach. A flat above a shop was not a maisonette. He tried to placate her and apologize to Mrs D at the same time.

Mrs D only made matters worse by saying, 'Yes, dear, you're only tenants.'

'We have been here five years,' Mrs Patel said – again via her husband – as though this made a difference to their position.

'And he's been here nine, dear.' Mrs D pointed at me.

Mrs Patel looked at me and snorted. Her husband signalled his apology to me behind her back.

'Who care where we go?' asked the Negro. It was how we all felt and what we had all so far avoided asking. Our unspoken answers were interrupted by the arrival of Atlas.

'Mr Muscles is here,' the Negro said in a low voice.

'What is it? More news about the eviction – the old kicking out?' Atlas said. After that it would have been difficult for any of us to have continued.

Mr Patel repeated part of his prepared speech for Atlas's benefit.

The Negro said, 'I think next time I make it to the Dorchester,' and Mrs D told him there was no need to adopt that attitude.

Mrs Patel had positioned her cup on her knee to indicate that she was thirsty. Her husband pulled a dozen tea bags from his pocket and presented them to Mrs D. We all thanked him. She dropped six into a tin and used the rest to make the tea. Being all together in such a confined space made me finally realize how little we all had in common.

Mrs Patel asked if it was true that I'd lived in the house nine years. I told her it was, wanting also to suggest that I had been previously unaware of the fact. She asked me where I'd lived before that. In his role as interpreter, her husband apologized for her inquisitiveness. I told her I'd been married. Behind her Mr Patel mouthed the word 'Divorce' and shook his head vigorously. He considered very carefully everything I said before translating it for her. She smiled when she should have frowned.

We were interrupted by the Negro who forced himself between us and helped himself to more tea. His girlfriend came to stand beside me.

'You're a writer,' she said.

'I try.'

She turned away to watch Mrs D take the teapot from the Negro.

'Sweetness,' she said absently. 'That's his name.'

'Nickname,' I corrected.

'From me.' She smiled at him and he watched us both suspiciously.

The Irishman and Atlas began a conversation which ended with them both pressing the palms of their hands together and grasping each other. The West Indians sat apart, pulling faces at the taste of the tea. Mrs D, taken with the idea of playing hostess, moved among us filling our cups.

Our meeting ended far less decisively than it had begun. Mr Patel began to say something, but no one listened. His wife tried unsuccessfully to shush us into silence. As we left he told me that he'd prepared some closing remarks and that they were every bit as good as his opening ones. I told him I believed him. He said that Churchill had been a great statesman.

'And a great liar,' I suggested.

'Oh, no no no no,' he said.

I apologized, followed him upstairs and stood with him on the landing as the others filed past us. Farouk, who had not been present at the meeting, came down to show off his new shirt. It was black with a pattern of silver moons and stars, over which he wore a white tie and his usual medallion.

'All men together,' said Mr Patel. His wife tutted and left us, and a minute later we also dispersed.

'There isn't the money,' she said. 'The chihuahuas.' She had abandoned breeding chihuahuas. We were in bed together. It was the middle of summer and uncomfortably warm at midnight.

'Get rid of them,' I suggested disinterestedly. They had never been a particularly easy dog to breed or care for. She said she should have done it years ago. She sounded depressed. The dogs were restless and irritable because of the heat. During the day we filled their water dishes every hour. She'd bought a child's inflatable paddling pool and put it in one of the compounds.

'The market's gone completely,' she said.

I lit a cigarette, blew rings into the half light and imagined how much happier she would have been with someone prepared to share her enthusiasm and her problems.

There were several nights at the height of summer when neither of us slept. I remember them clearly. She spoke of the dogs and I listened. She said she understood what I wanted, but it was a lie.

'Things can only get better,' she'd once said, not really believing it. I'd told her to keep thinking so. There had always been a peace of sorts between the wars.

After seeing her with the man in the bar I wondered if she'd slept with him in that same bed. The thought neither pleased nor upset me. I phoned her once, but put the receiver down before anyone answered.

A social worker had come into the house and Mrs D invested his arrival with an almost biblical significance. We gathered to meet him on the first floor landing.

'Social *scientist, ac*tually.' He handed round a plastic card of identification instead of shaking hands.

Mrs D asked him what the difference was. He explained. He was in the area doing research on the way people felt about the re-development. It was for his thesis, which he hoped eventually to work up into a book entitled *The Despair of Dislocation*. What did we feel?

'Despair,' said Atlas.

Mrs D said that she had been dislocated during the war – Central Line, Piccadilly, Victoria –

The Social Scientist said he didn't think that was quite the same thing and thereafter addressed his questions to the rest of us. The title had been thought up by his girlfriend, another Social Scientist.

'And what does she stick *her* nose into?' Atlas asked.

'Incest, *ac*tually.'

Mrs D asked what it was. Those of us who knew shared uneasy glances and drew mental straws to see who would tell her.

The situation was saved by Mrs Patel, who said 'Insects?' and waited for her husband to explain. The Social Scientist looked suddenly beaten.

Mrs D asked him if any of us would benefit from his work. He couldn't be sure but said that at the end of it all he'd have letters after his name and be entitled to call himself 'Doctor'. I waited for her to tell him about her back, or arms, or legs, or about the rash the sun gave her in summer, or the way her toes tingled in winter. He explained the difference to her.

'The truth is, you just want to know,' she said.

He said he didn't see anything wrong with that. None of us did. But, equally, none of us was prepared to let him succeed at what we considered to be our expense.

'The point is,' he said, 'if you don't find out how people are affected by these things, then it's never going to get any better.'

Mrs D wanted to know how she was expected to feel at having the house in which she'd lived woman and girl for fifty years pulled down around her ears.

He said it was a natural response.

'What was?'

Hostility.

Who was he calling hostile?

What he meant was –

Hostile! Her? Red Indians were hostile.

Statistics showed –

Coming into her house and treating her like that.

Mr Patel said that he personally was not hostile.

– that well over seventy per cent of all householders expressed some feeling of resentment at –

'Red, dear, *Red* Indians.' Exasperated.

If he already knew, then why was he here?

He waited until she'd finished and then apologized. From his briefcase he took a sheaf of questionnaires and asked us if we'd mind filling them in. He left us, promising to return that evening.

For the rest of the day Mrs D moved among us like an invigilator at an examination. We were asked to rate our feelings of uncertainty, despair, lack of identity and rootlessness along a scale of one to ten. Atlas was the first to finish. Mr Patel spent hours explaining the questions to his wife and then trying to understand them himself. I told him that seldom in the field of urban renewal had so much been expected of so few with so little idea of how much was actually happening. He said he understood my concern and confessed that he'd marked his own uncertain feelings from four to six in each instance. He didn't know what he felt and didn't want to spoil the man's chance of success. Mrs D said she hoped none of this would reflect badly on her. I pointed out that we were not required to give our names or address on the form.

At seven the Social Scientist returned and we gave him our forms. Mrs D handed hers over in a sealed envelope. He said there was no need. She said you couldn't be too careful. Mrs Patel came down the stairs and held out her cupped hands to the man, opening them to reveal a silverfish. She spoke to her husband, who looked immediately embarrassed.

'An insect,' he said. 'She thought . . .'

Mrs D told the researcher that there had never been anything like *that* in the house before the demolition work began. It was a lie, of course, but he was in no position to argue. She said smugly that she didn't suppose there would be room in his book for that kind of thing. He said he doubted it.

'No, well . . .' Her position was unassailable.

Then the Irishman came down with his form on which he had written nothing. He asked for a pen and went quickly through it, ticking and crossing and circling, with Mrs D trying to look over his shoulder.

The researcher asked us when we expected to leave. Mrs D announced that she'd expected to die in the house. The rest of us guessed at a likely date.

'Will you get the book, do you think?' the Irishman asked.

The man shrugged. 'To tell you the truth, I'd hoped for a more forceful and widespread expression of despair.'

With that he left us.

'At least it's something,' the Irishman said, as though we had in some way benefited from the brief encounter.

In the street someone shouted. I looked out and saw a man running past. Downstairs Mrs D and the Irishman came out of her room and stood in the doorway. I asked them what was happening. The Irishman shook his head. I went out into the street and he led her back inside.

At the end of the street a small crowd had gathered. Standing apart from them, with his hands on the shoulders of a crying woman, was one of the demolition workers. Beyond them I saw that the top third of the mural had already been destroyed. As I watched, the jib of a small crane swung silently towards it. More of the wall crumpled and fell.

The running man arrived beside me. 'They can't do that,' he said calmly, as though believing he had the power to remedy what was happening. I pointed to the obvious.

Barriers had been erected, and beyond them the rest of the wall collapsed and settled in clouds of dust. The interior outline of a house was revealed in a pattern of hearths and staircases and squares of wallpaper. Beyond that there was only sky and the distant horizon of weatherstained tower blocks.

For several minutes chunks of scenery continued to topple down. The sky was reduced, and then the buildings and market stalls. As they fell the bricks came apart like the pieces of a jigsaw and piled up in a scree at the foot of the wall. There were figures at the very bottom of the mural which the swinging lead ball couldn't reach, and which stood among the rubble like the survivors of an earthquake. When the demolition was completed, the youths who had painted the wall began to cheer. I looked for the artist but he wasn't among them. Some of them pushed through the barriers and sought out individual bricks as souvenirs.

The crane driver climbed from his cab and bowed to the crowd.

When I returned to the house Mrs D and the Irishman were still together in her room.

'It's a shock she's had,' he said. She held his bottle, and when she raised it to drink he watched it rather than her.

'There was never much chance of it not being demolished,' I said.

'Bastards,' she said. 'The rotten bastards.'

The Irishman turned to me and shrugged. 'It's the shock,' he said again. It was only his half-filled bottle which kept him there.

'They painted it on purpose,' she said. 'They lied.'

'No one lied. All they wanted –'

'They lied!' She looked up at me and swore again.

The Irishman flinched. 'You've had a shock, that's all,' he said. 'Why don't I . . . ?' He knelt to try and retrieve his bottle, reaching towards it as though it were a snake and might suddenly strike out at him. 'Why don't I just . . .?'

'Why don't you just mind your own fuckin' business.' It was the first time I'd ever heard her use the word. She was drunk. It shouldn't have surprised me, but it did. She looked up at me and I thought she was about to apologize. 'Why don't the pair of you mind your own fuckin' business. Go on, get out. Out!'

Neither of us moved. Me because I didn't know what to do; the Irishman because he had not yet rescued his bottle. The room was cold. I knelt and lit the fire.

'That's it,' he said to her. 'You need warming up.'

I wanted him to leave. I drew the curtains. Across the road a line of heavy machinery had drawn up and was manoeuvring over the waste ground, bouncing beams of light over the uneven surface and filling the cold air with a white cloud of exhaust fumes.

'I'll have to be getting off soon,' the Irishman said, still gesturing towards the bottle.

'Go then.' She turned towards the fire and slid the bottle between her feet.

'We'll leave you,' I said.

She nodded and then shook her head. 'Not you, just Irish.'

I saw him tense. The fire burned with a rasping sound and the flames rose and fell unevenly.

'They're tampering with the gas,' she said.

I looked to the Irishman to see if he thought that likely.

'Might be. You'll all be on the same main,' he said.

She asked him for a cigarette. He gave her one and sat down beside her. She handed him the bottle. He drank from it, passed it to me and then back to her.

'You're trying to get me drunk,' she said. 'The pair of you.' She giggled. 'You'll take advantage. A girl isn't safe.'

The Irishman put his arm around her shoulders.

'You stay too,' she said, and patted the sofa on the other side of her. I sat down and saw our three reflections in the rear window.

'I'll draw the other curtains,' I said.

'You do that.'

As I rose she turned to the Irishman and repeated what she'd said about being taken advantage of. He said he wouldn't dream of it and they both fell back laughing. He kissed her on the cheek and she pushed him away. From the high mantelpiece her two husbands looked down at us. There was a slight fall of soot around the fire. She said she should have had the chimney cleaned before blocking it up. Behind the fire the sheet of hardboard was broken and scorched. She dipped the tips of her fingers into the hearth and left black dots along the Irishman's arm. He told her to stop and then rubbed at them with his sleeve.

'Touchy,' she said, and then offered him the last of his drink. He stared at it before swallowing it.

'We're all in this together,' she suddenly announced, and we all fell silent.

A few minutes later the front door opened and music filled the hall. We listened as it moved up the stairs.

'One of the darkies,' the Irishman said.

'They're all darkies,' she said, studying the neck of the empty bottle. 'You can call them what you want, but that's what they are.'

The music rose to the top of the house.

'They're going soon,' she said.

'The West Indians?'

'The darkies in the attic. Next week. Four years they've been here.' She made their departure sound as though it was the result of something she'd said or done to offend them.

'It's a long time,' the Irishman said.

'It is. A long time. If I had my time again . . .' If she had her time again she would fill the house with single, professional gentlemen – doctors, lawyers, City men. And in the midst of them she would become something completely different from the woman she had become in the midst of us. I understood all this, but I doubted if the Irishman did.

'There'd be no room for the likes of me in the scheme of things,' he said.

She smiled at him as though in his case she would consider making an exception. He told her that he wouldn't expect to be able to live with her if things were any different.

'No offence,' she said.

'It's always the way of things,' he said. He stroked her arm and kissed her again. She seemed not to notice. He put the mouth of the empty bottle to her lips and she blew into it.

'There'd be a sink and a decent bed in every room,' she said.

'There would that.'

'And meals. A proper dining room.' She looked round the room and saw it as it would have been.

'It's the shock,' he said to me.

'The shock,' she repeated.

I sat back down beside her. The Irishman swayed forward and rested his forehead on her knees. She placed a hand on his neck.

'He's been drinking all dinner,' she said. She stroked his shoulder. 'All Micks drink too much. Well known for it. He ought to be in bed.'

I offered to help him up to his room. She said it didn't matter, released his head and let it fall against the arm of the sofa. He opened his eyes, said 'What?' and then closed them again. A few seconds later he began to snore. She held up his bottle to the light to make sure it was empty. 'Dead,' she said, and then, 'just me and you now.' Me and her and a house full of darkies.

We lifted the Irishman's legs on to the sofa and took off his shoes. She looked at the holes in his socks and said she felt sorry for him.

The house is being dismantled, slate by slate, brick by brick, board by board, from chimney to cellar, bought by an American to be shipped to America and rebuilt. We may travel with it, or we may not. Mrs D will not. Wild horses wouldn't drag her to America. The house will be rebuilt in a dry climate, perhaps in a small desert. There will be ropes to guide visitors and a peep-show arcade where it will be possible to witness life as it was lived in the house. Everything will be sprayed with a protective plastic coating and will need to be dusted only once a week. No attempt will be made to reproduce the garden in all its splendour. The garden belongs to another age, ancient as opposed to modern history. The figures, if willing, might be embalmed or reproduced in wax with real hair and the clothing as worn by the actual people. Us. Only the mortar between the bricks and the nails in the wood will not be re-used. These will be sold as souvenirs to finance the operation. There will be a tape of familiar sounds repeated every hour on the hour and played through hidden speakers. Entrance will be free.

Mrs D supervises the demolition. The men wear gloves, chipping and brushing like archaeologists excavating a tomb. She watches and directs them. It does her heart good. Every piece is labelled and listed, drawn, measured and numbered, crated up, padded and carted away. At night, spotlights are erected and the work continues. Guards are posted.

We are asked for our reminiscences of the house and for any old photographs we might have of it. Mrs D sells memories of her mother and husbands. She regrets having told us so much. Our second-hand information forces down the price of her own more valuable recollections. Everything we say is cross-checked and filed. The museum will be the most complete of its kind. There are even scientists working on ways of reproducing the distinctive smells of each room. Waste is collected from the drains and plumbing, dust from beneath the beds. The shapes of furniture are chalked on to the carpets, pictures outlined in pencil against the carefully removed wallpaper. Nothing will escape. Mrs D reconsiders the offer to accompany the house. She will become a national figure. The idea appeals. She turns it down. The price paid for her husbands is doubled. The grass and sediment from the guttering is taken away in plastic bags. Cushions of moss are sliced from the flaking sills and lintels. Nothing is lost.

When the work is complete we are left only with an outline into which rubble from the adjoining houses has already fallen. Mrs D returns to comfort us. The Americans have presented her with copies of the portraits of her husbands; the originals are already beyond reach.

Now it is over, only the Patels and Farouk seem genuinely pleased at what has happened. The Negro and his girl have bought a car with their share of the money. They circle the streets blowing the horn.

'Flashy,' says Mrs D. Money brought people out in their true light.

On the waste land one of the tramps has been found dead. Mrs D went from room to room announcing that the police had arrived to question us. She continued to live in a state of permanent crisis. A death. She had known all along that it would come to this.

The two policemen waited in the hallway. They breathed the house's smells and screwed up their noses. Because no one else was willing, I accompanied her back downstairs. She introduced me to them and they asked me my full name, the extent of the view from my window, and my occupation. I told them I was unemployed and that the tramp's body would have been visible from my window had it been distinguishable from the mounds of rubble and litter amid which it had been found. Mrs D considered this a good answer and nodded vigorously. The policemen simply thought I was being clever. She said she personally had neither heard nor seen anything. One of the constables remarked that he thought all the houses of this terrace had been abandoned weeks ago. The other asked if I'd mind them accompanying me to my room. 'To assess what might or might not be visible from it. Sir.'

Mrs D and I preceded them upstairs.

In my room they examined the papers on the desk and then drew back the curtains to look out over the expanse of mud and rubble and snow on which the body had been found.

'And you neither heard nor saw anything, sir?'

'When?'

They weren't sure. They asked how long the land had been in that condition and how long the tramps had been there. One of them continued to make notes while the other asked Mrs D about the rest of her tenants. She answered him with her hand over her heart.

When they'd gone she called them names and we returned downstairs together.

In addition to the tree and streamers in the hallway she had decorated her own room, draping gold tinsel around each of her husbands. Beside them was an advent calendar with all its doors already open. When I remarked on this, she said that there didn't seem to be any point in waiting, that the pictures were the same every year. On the table was the remains of a meal. She said she'd let things slip. I wondered if what the Irishman had told me about her husbands was true and asked her if they were in fact buried in the local cemetery. She said they were, but that she seldom visited them. 'Neither of them had any other family, see.'

Everything she said about them sounded rehearsed.

She concluded with the dates and causes of their deaths. 'Both peaceful, both at home.' She wouldn't have seen either of them suffer.

She carried the plate from the table into the kitchen alcove.

'Neither of them liked Christmas much,' she said. 'Too pissed to notice most years. Always a nice present, though, always that.' She ran a hand around her cheap necklaces, and I knew then precisely what kind of men they had been and why she encouraged the advances of the Irishman and the men in the bars. 'They knew how to enjoy themselves,' she continued, excusing their drunkenness just as she excused the Irishman's. 'They were different days.'

She made me think of my four Christmases with Lynette, and of her refusal to interrupt the daily routine of cleaning the kennels. She felt betrayed because the kennel-maids demanded two, sometimes three consecutive days' holiday. She refused to pay them a bonus. Instead she bought each of the dogs a new jacket or collar, a bowl or toy. I always received disappointing clothes or toiletries, for which I pretended to be grateful. The dogs came into the house, and what remained of the turkey was fed to them during the afternoon and evening. We spent Boxing Day at her mother's, always leaving mid-afternoon for Lynette to attend to the dogs. Every year the same.

'You don't make much of an effort yourself,' Mrs D said. 'Christmas, I mean.'

I told her I didn't think there was much point, especially not this Christmas.

'Oh, there's always a point to things. Just because . . .'

I wondered if she really believed it, or whether she'd said it simply to hear me tell her she was right. I told her she was and she looked pleased.

Indicating her husbands, she said, 'They were like you. They could never understand the effort. But I always saw to it that we made something of it.'

I told her we all appreciated her decorations. This pleased her even more and she asked me what the others had said. I told her about the Patels' decorations. She said she supposed they'd bought everything new. We were describing two completely different occasions: something which was happening now and something which had happened a quarter of a century ago. The present could only have appeared tawdry and hopeless by comparison. It was the difference between what she had become and a time when every opportunity was still open to her. She wiped her eyes and said that the policemen and the death of the tramp had upset her.

I left her and stood outside her door. She switched on her radio and turned the dial until the room was filled with voices singing hymns.

The following morning two men arrived with a lorry to remove Mrs D's furniture. Another crisis. She had expected them to come on the day of our departure and they were here now, more than a fortnight early. Her belongings will be put into storage in the basement of her new home.

I spoke to them for her, explaining the situation. They threatened to leave. They were angry. Shifting furniture wasn't their job. Tree felling was their normal job. They were shifting the furniture as a favour for someone else. I pointed out that all the local trees had long since been felled. The driver said, 'As you like,' and started the engine. I apologized and told them to collect the furniture. They followed me indoors and past Mrs D.

They cleared the hallway of piled boxes. Mrs D moved from one to the other, indicating what they should take and what was to stay. She suggested a cup of tea and both men sat down before she had finished filling the kettle. They became friendlier and ready to sympathize with her. She wanted to know who would help her move her belongings from the basement into her new home. She said she had never lived anywhere with a basement before, only ever cellars. Neither of them knew. It was in a different borough. They drank her tea and told her it was a shame she was being forced to leave so close to Christmas. She introduced them to her husbands. I joined them, but had clearly already been branded as a trouble-maker by the men and a failed negotiator by Mrs D. The older man said he shouldn't be lifting furniture and rubbed his chest. When they eventually went back outside I told her they would expect a tip. She said it was their job. I told her about the trees. She looked alarmed and pushed her purse deep into the pocket of her apron.

I watched one of the men screw a tab end into the hallway carpet with his foot.

When they had finished Mrs D went out to look at her possessions crowded into one corner of their lorry. She seemed surprised that they took up so little space.

The men returned, expecting to be tipped.

I said, 'What about the carpets, Mrs D?' Both men glared at me. She studied the worn, almost patternless carpet on which we stood. One of the men said that he thought a lot of the new houses were already fitted with carpet tiles. The idea appealed to her and she began speculating on the likely colours. The men encouraged her. She followed them out to their cab, took out her purse and gave them something, coins rather than notes – not for what they had congrudgingly done, but because they'd raised her expectations concerning the carpets.

On her return she picked up the small silver tree from the hallway and brought it into her room. I helped her rearrange what little furniture remained around the fire. She said she would pack what was left of her belongings on the night before she finally went. There were her clothes and knick-knacks, her cutlery, jewellery, photographs and memories. She stood the tree on the kitchen table, picking its silver needles off her sleeve.

Looking up at the high ceiling, she said, 'Weeks, that's all,' and announced almost proudly that there was no one living in the six houses on either side of us. None of them, she said, had waited for Christmas in their own homes. She had known some of her neighbours all the time she'd lived there. Some had called in to say their farewells, but most had simply gone. They were all guilty of something of which she alone was blameless. She asked me if I knew when the houses had been built. I guessed at a hundred years ago and she agreed.

An hour after the departure of the two men it started to snow again. One half of the sky was of the palest blue, the other almost black. We looked out together and she asked me if I thought the two men would unload her belongings in the snow. I said I doubted it. She said they looked to her like the kind of men who would unload someone else's belongings in the snow.

With the overcast sky it became as dark as evening at midday.

We heard the Irishman come down the stairs and she stood behind her door with her finger to her lips until he'd gone. When the front door slammed behind him she let out her breath and waited.

'He's getting a bit too . . .' She held an imaginary glass to her mouth. She meant much more.

I watched him through the window. He gave money to a man on the street and then shouted to another on the opposite pavement.

'He's not a bad man really,' she said.

'No, I don't suppose he is.'

'Hard times.' She mouthed the words rather than spoke them.

'Force of circumstance,' I said, and she smiled at what she believed to be our shared understanding.

She asked me if the Irishman had told me of his own plans. I said he hadn't and we sat together until the snow stopped and was followed by rain.

Now, as always, there are days when I go no further from my room than the landing or bathroom. The sound of opening doors acts as a signal. Someone is waiting on my return. The Irishman has spent a full night asleep on the bed of one of the empty rooms. He came in drunk and got no further than the second landing. It no longer matters. He arrives at the smell of cooking. He eats his own meals in bars between his drinks, and before and after the dull voids of which most of our days are composed. An earthquake might be about to open up the ground and claim us, or a volcano explode and drown us in ash. We will petrify and rot and become as insubstantial as the spaces we now inhabit. We are responsive to nothing but the pressing moment. Our days are filled with small urgencies. Occasionally the Irishman returns with one of his drinking friends. They sit in his room and sing until the early hours. The nights are clear and empty and everything is illuminated by the cold glare of the moon. Mr Patel refuses to discuss his brother-in-law. His wife screams at him, slapping her stomach to punish him. Heavy lorries clear the rubble and shake the house.

Birds still scavenge over the more recently demolished sites. Beyond the cemetery a Victorian church and vicarage have been destroyed. Broken statues and gargoyles stand among the ruins like garden gnomes in a rockery.

We tore off her blouse and she screamed, her mouth growing wider and wider until any one of us might have fallen into it. We froze. Anyone might have heard. She had never screamed before, not even when I began slashing at her with the blade. Then she had only winced and held back the sound, as though she had been receiving a feared but necessary injection prior to an otherwise greater pain. She surprised even herself, stopped struggling and remained silent. Mr Patel shook her. Mrs Patel resumed her chanting. The mouth closed and she waited for me to continue. She didn't actually speak, but I saw in her eyes that it was what she wanted. A mistake had been made. I awoke and was drawn back. An empty train rattled through the underground. When the dream returned only the aftermath remained. I had left it and then returned to it. The knife was still in my hand, but someone else had killed her during my absence. I demanded to know who. They looked at me, surprised. I had ruined the final scene. The body on the ground grumbled, stood up, and pulled on its clothes. The others apologized to her and cast angry glances at me. I shouted to them but my mouth felt numb and the words refused to form. Mrs D said I'd made a big enough fool of myself so why didn't I just keep quiet. There was blood on the knife in my hand, but no sign of it or a wound on her.

The following night the dream returned and an order of sorts was re-established.

But whatever the dream might once have been to me, it no longer suggested a way ahead. Like much of what else we all now said and did, it had become a reflex, a spasm of tightening muscle prior to stillness.

I awoke in the darkness and felt pleased with myself. The room took shape around me. Years ago there had been a midnight-shift-change whistle and another at six in the morning, both of them miles away but clearly audible when the wind was in the right direction. In between had been the quarterly chimings of a number of church clocks. They too had long since fallen silent.

My insomnia persists and is a direct result of my lethargy. I do not need to exert myself physically and so cannot exhaust myself sufficiently to sleep.

There are nights and early mornings when I wake shaking. At other times I can remember nothing of the dream, only that it has taken place.

I wonder on occasion whether or not my ulcer might have returned. Having been unable to locate it by feeling, I tried to visualize it. The best I could do was to see it as a spotlessly clean, pearly white and perfectly formed button mushroom. When I thought of it, it worried me. The doctor had told me that if it did return it would respond adversely to alcohol. I continued to drink and wait. The vision of it seemed to come to me too easily for it *not* to exist. I half expected the dream to reveal something similar inside Mrs D, shining out at me from the flesh which peeled apart so easily at the point of the knife. Nothing has yet appeared. It is largely because these connections are not made that I persist in thinking of the dream and the motivation behind it as being separate entities. I am not responsible, and therefore powerless to do anything but participate and wait for it to end.

The light at the window is grey, broken by passing headlights. In summer it is light well before six, at the height of summer before five.

Mr Patel stands dressed completely in white, his jacket to his knees, his brown shins and bare feet exposed. His wife and children stand beside him, similarly dressed. They are going home to India and have come to pay their last respects. She is holding a baby and is once again slim, young and attractive. They stand with their palms together, smiling benevolently. They offer to take me with them. I have no time for them and tell them so. I demand to know why they are leaving so suddenly. They refuse to answer me. One dream follows another.

I used to lie awake and listen for the six o'clock whistle. The day began as part of someone else's routine. The wind was in the right direction. The Irishman said that from his own home he could hear and see the ships on the river. As a child he had watched them glide noiselessly between the houses. He wishes he'd been a seaman. It would have suited him.

'You disgust me.'

'I disgust you.'

She ignored me and continued measuring out the dogs' food. 'You got drunk deliberately. You insulted everybody and made me look a fool.'

'You forget how much practice I've had.'

We had been to her mother's for a meal. Her parents were celebrating their fortieth wedding anniversary. Lynette gave them a silver plate which she'd had engraved. From A Loving Daughter and Son-in-Law. Most of the other members of the family had also been present. Several of the men refused to drink on the grounds that they were driving. Their wives smiled at them as though they were clever children. Lynette's father said he was pleased to see me and shook my hand. I said forty years was a long time. He said I'd find out. I wanted to tell him that I doubted it. Events were to prove me right. There was less than a month to go before our final separation.

Lynette opened a bottle of champagne and everyone cheered. Her mother explained to them that we – Lynette and I – were used to celebrating. She meant the dogs but tried to make it sound like something more. The cracks were too wide not to be showing. Even the non-drinking men took shallow glasses and sipped at the champagne as though it were a strong spirit. The women began saying how it made them feel giddy and reckless before they'd even tasted it. There hadn't been a reckless member of the family for generations. It had been bred out of them.

The conversation moved around the room. I said something – I can't remember what – and everyone fell silent. Lynette tried to explain it away. People laughed politely.

I went upstairs to the bathroom and stood looking out over the line of immaculately kept gardens behind the houses. There was a strong smell of lavender. I opened the window and shouted out at the top of my voice. Several neighbours turned to look, but no one saw me. It wasn't a shouting neighbourhood. I rinsed my face in the sink.

When I went back downstairs the women were passing around photograph albums, demanding to be shown the pictures of themselves and then insisting that everyone else should see them. Lynette's mother studied herself as a girl and began to cry. The others comforted her. She started to say something about her non-existent grandchildren and stopped. I heard myself tell her to mind her own business.

On the way home I fell asleep in the car, waking only as we arrived alongside the kennels. Lynette said I'd embarrassed her and made myself look a fool. She said she'd intended leaving me in the car. I'd ruined everything. Forty years down the drain. A month left.

It was Sunday and neither of the kennel-maids was in. The dogs leapt up at the metal bowls as she laid them along the runs. She watched them and said she didn't know why we bothered. I asked her what she meant. She said 'Nothing', and walked away. I stayed where I was, watching her at the far end of the garden.

After their meal the dogs gathered around her. I went into the house and watched her from my small upstairs room. She played with the dogs, and those confined to their pens ran and threw themselves against the mesh in their excitement. She threw rubber balls to them and stood looking out over the waste land. It was a warm day and the field and distant houses shimmered in the heat. The dogs formed into groups and chased each other up and down the compounds until they were exhausted. I waited until I saw her return to the house before going downstairs.

She brushed one of the poodles and said that things had gone on for long enough.

'Things?'

She said I knew what she meant.

Outside the dogs had grown quiet, worn out by their running and the heat. They lay around their pens in the triangles of shadow. The dog she was brushing stood in her lap and panted. She trimmed the hair over its eyes and ears.

Later, in the evening, the house became suddenly cold, and filled with the lurid glare of the setting sun. She went out to secure the kennels for the night. I followed and spoke to her, but she refused to answer. The sun sank into the horizon beyond the field and houses, melting whatever it touched. She tightened the scarf around her neck and held herself. I saw something in her I'd never seen before, and which, until then, I would have denied existed. She had resigned herself to what would now happen to us.

There was a show the following weekend and she began to speculate on the chances of the entered dogs.

The Negro and his girl sat on the swings in the empty playground. He sat slumped forward and she held the chains and rocked him. He looked up at my approach but said nothing. I sat beside her and told her I was on my way to see another flat. She asked me about it but listened without interest as I read out the advertisement. Occasionally, the Negro lifted his head with his eyes closed and said something to her. She indicated to me not to try and speak to him, holding out his tobacco tin in explanation. His hair fell over his face and hid it completely. I asked her if either of them had found anywhere to go. She said they hadn't. The playground fence had been uprooted the previous week and the ground was littered with bricks. I asked her if she would be able to get him home. She shook her head and said she'd wait until he felt better. I left them and walked through the playground and past the gypsy caravans.

The flat was nothing more than two attic rooms, poorly furnished and badly decorated, at the top of a house overlooking a school and its playing fields. The couple who owned the house went with me into the rooms and outlined the terms of the tenancy. They asked me where I was moving from, and when I told them they exchanged knowing looks.

'Everyone else in the house is in full employment,' the woman said. She tugged at her earrings.

Every time her husband spoke he cleared his throat first. He began to list the professions of their other tenants on his fingers.

'Paying guests,' she corrected.

'Paying guests. Two council operatives –'

'Cleansing and Disposal Management.'

'Someone' – pause – 'in the City, who –'

'Clerk to a legal man.'

They smiled together as though he were their son.

'A very nice lady in the clothing trade.'

'Select lines . . . Nothing . . .' She looked from my collar to my shoes.

'Waiting for the right openings.'

'Premises of her own.'

And a philatelic gentleman beneath me.

'Stamp dealer.'

'Not on the premises, you understand.'

I understood.

'No, certainly not.'

They shared a nervous smile and asked me what I did. I told them I'd expected something larger and better furnished.

I walked back through the playground, but the Negro and his girl had gone.

In the hallway Mrs D introduced me to a girl rocking a baby in a pram. She told me her name. The baby cried.

'Looking for a room,' Mrs D said. 'I was telling her what a pity I'd none left.'

The girl tried to calm the baby.

'Poor mite,' Mrs D said.

'Teething,' the girl said. She'd looked all over. The house in which she lived was being pulled down in a fortnight. Mrs D said it was coming to us all. The cries of the teething baby filled the house. She helped the girl lift the pram down the steps and waggled her finger in the baby's face. I waited for her to return.

'You know what that was, don't you?' she said.

I told her I didn't.

'A one-parent family.'

I wondered if any of them anywhere ever led comfortable lives.

In *her* day there had only been unmarried mothers.

In her day there had been change from a shilling after buying almost anything you cared to mention, and decent, honest people had lived with other decent, honest people. They might never have had much, but they were decent and honest and lived by the sweat of their brows.

I refused to be drawn. Earlier in the day she'd had an enquiry from an old German couple ('Left over from the war'). There were lines on the carpet from the pram. I heard music from the Negro's room.

'You could have let her have a room for a few weeks,' I suggested.

She stared at me disbelievingly. She said she supposed I approved of that kind of thing. I cared as much for the homeless girl and her teething baby as she did. I left her and she shouted after me. I shouted back.

The music grew louder until it was all there was, until it enveloped me and shook the house to its foundations, until even thinking became impossible, until Mrs D and the baby opened their mouths and all that came out was the music.

Farouk has been arrested and released. Two detectives were waiting for him as he left work. The owner of the club held his arm and handed him over. All this is his story. The owner hailed the police car as though it were a taxi. Farouk said he felt the man's grip tighten and understood only then what was happening. I guessed by the tone of his voice as he told me that he had resigned himself to such an occurrence long ago. At the police station the detectives interviewed him and swore at him and 'his friends' for wasting their time. He was questioned, thanked, warned, released. In addition to which, he had been fired from the club, having worked all the previous day and night.

On the steps of the police station two men stood on either side of the doorway and watched as he came out. He has not been back to the club for the money he is owed and he is frightened. I tried to convince him that a genuine mistake had been made and that the detectives had simply been prejudiced.

'Because of what I am,' he said quietly.

I could understand his anxiety.

Then he cursed and shook his head. 'Always problems.'

I asked him if he was aware of anything more specific. We both knew what I meant and I was more embarrassed about asking than he was about answering. When he couldn't decide I suggested that someone at the club might have felt cheated and complained.

'They are all cheated. The men who go in that place would not complain to the police.' He lit a cigarette and sat with his hands splayed on the table. The room around him was as dark and cold as my own. I asked him if he thought the men on the station steps were in some way connected with what had happened. He said he didn't know, but that it seemed like too great a coincidence for them not to have been. I offered to phone the club and enquire about his money.

He asked me not to. I left him and heard him draw the chain on the door behind me.

Later that evening two men came to the house. They announced themselves as detectives and went to Farouk's room. I heard them knock at his door and go in. A few minutes later they left alone. I went up to see him but he refused to let me in. I asked him what they had wanted. He told me a mistake had been made and that they had called to apologize. He said he was tired and wanted to sleep.

In the morning I went back up. This time he let me in.

He was wearing pyjamas and an overcoat. The curtains were still drawn and the room smelt strongly of him and the cigarette smoke which still clouded it. On the table were several empty packets and a plate filled with ash and stubs. When he turned to face me in the half light I saw that he had a bruise across his nose and forehead, a slender cut stretching from the corner of his eye to his lips, and that one of his eyes was closed and swollen. It was not a bad cut, deep enough only to draw blood and looking worse than it was. His hair was wet and combed back. Beside him on the floor was the shirt with which he had wiped himself.

'They said they were policemen,' he said, sighing at his own stupidity.

I asked if he had any sticking plasters or cream for the bruise. He said he hadn't and that it didn't matter. The only injury which still caused him pain was his swollen eye. He touched it and flinched. I asked him who they were and he told me it was none of my business, that he recognized them from the club. He seemed to have accepted what had happened, so I pursued it no further. I switched on his fire and plugged in the kettle. He held the cup with both hands and smiled after the first mouthful as though his troubles were over.

'You won't go back to the club?'

He nodded towards his pillow, upon which were scattered five-pound notes. 'They threatened me. My sort . . .'

I told him there was no need to explain.

'Only to them.'

Around the walls were hung his collection of colourful shirts and jackets, each matched and buttoned, and with their collars neatly folded down. Some still hung in their plastic dry-cleaning bags. He picked up the shirt from the floor and said it was ruined. I pointed out that he had many others, equally smart. He chose one of his favourites and held it to his chest. Then he took off his overcoat and pyjamas and began to dress. He pulled on his socks and stood otherwise naked at the centre of the room. He stood with his back to me and studied his cut cheek in the mirror. His body seemed to darken from top to bottom. There was hair on his shoulders, and his buttocks were creamy, almost white. He turned to face me, rubbing his chest and arms, cupping his genitals and shaking them. There were other bruises on his stomach and thighs. He pulled on the shirt and sat beside me, turning the shadow of his crotch towards the fire and opening his legs until they were positioned on either side of it. On the back of his door was pinned a page from a Sunday magazine showing a collection of cracked and tinted photographs in which naked boys held each other's hands and faces. Their bodies were posed, their faces blank. Their organs were flaccid but enlarged. Behind them were backcloths of mountains and Indian temples. His shoes stood in pairs on newspaper beside the door leading to the fire escape, each pair polished and with its laces pulled to exact lengths. I counted eleven pairs. Beside them stood a box of polishes and cloths. I asked him how he intended spending the day. He shrugged and nodded towards the bed and the cigarettes on the table. He told me how much he'd enjoyed our day at the zoo, referring to it as though it had happened in the far distant past.

'We could always go again,' I suggested.

He shook his head. When he stood and yawned the shirt rose back to his stomach and he brushed at his shins where they had been too close to the fire.

'They think I am working,' he said. He meant his family. 'To them it is no different.'

I said he would get another job.

He chose a jacket from the wall. Once dressed he studied himself again in the mirror. From a drawer in the table he took out a card of six velvet bow ties. He chose a maroon one and slid its elastic beneath his collar, adjusting it until it sat level. Then he chose a pair of shoes and put them on. He moved across the room and drew back the curtains. He asked me what time it was. I guessed at midday.

I left him sitting at the table with a cold cloth to his eye. Where it touched his lips the cut had reopened and had started to bleed. He wiped the blood into his mouth with his thumb.

Mrs D is shouting. Everyone is shouting. I resist the urge to shout back and silence them. The doors to the house's empty rooms are constantly open. The front door is seldom locked. People come and go at all hours of the day and night. Our routine, the routine of the house, no longer exists. Those of us who remain are more careful of what we do and say. The staircases and corridors are lined with boxes and piles of newspapers waist high. Mrs D will fall and break her neck, fall and be left undiscovered for days. No one cares.

She shouts my name, always mine. I close my eyes and wait. She shouts again. I shout back and climb the stairs towards the noise. The Negro and his girl stand at their door. 'Better run,' he says. They both laugh. Because they are watching me I try not to hurry. By now her shouts are uncontrollable screams. She sounds once again like a bad actress in a Victorian music-hall melodrama.

On the third landing all the doors are open, the rooms empty. The street lights cast rectangles of light over their ceilings. Mrs D looks down from the attic rooms. The West Indians left yesterday. After four happy comfortable years they deserted her, her children, without a tear or a word of farewell. It was all the thanks she got.

I call up to her and she appears with her hands clasped in prayer in front of her face. I ask her what's wrong. She points into the room behind her. I want to calm her down but cannot bring myself to touch her. She wipes her face on her sleeve and pushes me into the room ahead of her. It is completely bare, stripped naked. Even the linoleum and curtain rails have gone. There is no light bulb, no cord hanging from the ceiling. The switch by the door is a square of plaster and exposed wiring.

'The dirty, rotten, thieving bastards,' she says. 'The dirty, rotten . . .' Thieving bastards. Apparently. She says it as though she has suspected it all along. They have taken everything. I do my best not to laugh. I am there to prove her right and support her prejudices.

'Call the police,' I suggest, silencing her.

I walk into the room and she waits behind me at the door. I inspect it by the light of matches. The two skylights have been propped open. I pull them shut and realize only then that even the glass has been removed and that the screws have been taken from the hinges. The empty frames fall into the room and smash.

'The glass,' I say. 'They've taken everything.' I enjoy saying it. I knew from previous visits that the room had never contained much furniture, and that even this had been the shabbiest she possessed.

But its removal had been much more than theft. Less than murder, but calculatingly close. The tiles had been chipped from the disused fireplace and remained scattered in the hearth. On one wall they had even begun to scrape away at the wallpaper. I stood with my back to her. She was breathing deeply, supporting herself against the wall. She'd had a shock. It could have killed her. It might yet kill her. Who cared? If she had screamed again I would have left her in the doorway and gone downstairs.

Mr and Mrs Patel stood on the landing below and shouted up. I left the room, telling her there was nothing any of us could do. She said she'd intended taking the furniture with her, thus creating a greater tragedy than already existed.

We descended the stairs together, and on the second-floor landing she suddenly stopped and ran to the low cupboard which held the electricity meters. She inspected them, sighed dramatically and once again held the wall to steady herself.

'I had no idea,' I said.

'No.' We were all being accused. Rain splashed against the window and bleared our reflections.

'And I don't suppose any of you heard a thing,' she said sarcastically.

'We . . .' Whatever I said would have made no difference.

'The dirty, rotten, thieving bastards took everything. Everything. The lot!' Her words returned in a vague echo.

Mr and Mrs Patel appeared ahead of us and stood by their own door. I asked Mrs Patel how she was, pointing to her stomach. She looked down, puzzled, and then began a rapid monologue which only she and her husband understood.

'She's expecting,' I said to Mrs D.

She nodded. 'They always are.' I wondered if she'd intended the remark to sound as cruel as it did.

Mrs Patel traced the outline of her stomach with her thumb, pressing around its lower edge.

'Very nice, dear.'

Mrs Patel bowed.

'Are you going to call the police?'

She'd had enough of them over the previous months.

'They might –'

'They might come and have a good laugh – that's what *they* might do!' She was a poor, defenceless old woman and nobody cared. She moved ahead of me down the stairs.

Many of the neighbouring houses had been demolished with a good deal of considerably better furniture still in place and with carpets which fell and covered their broken floors.

She turned and said that none of this would have happened if either of her husbands had been alive. *They* would have protected her. She was referring to much more than the theft of the furniture and destruction of the room. Her husbands were better men than the street had known since. She descended the remaining stairs muttering loudly to herself.

Two streets away three old brothers have barricaded themselves inside the house in which their grandfather was born. All three are old soldiers, widowers, and were, they said, well prepared for siege. The house had been boarded up and was believed empty until one, the youngest at seventy-three, began to shout down to passers-by through a hand-made megaphone. The police arrived, an ambulance arrived, newspaper reporters arrived. A local councillor arrived and asked them to be reasonable. He was pelted with something indeterminate and retreated out of range. An hour later he returned with two other councillors and repeated what he'd said before about being civilized, reasonable men. He was pelted again and all three ran and crouched behind their car. The small crowd of onlookers cheered. I stood with Farouk, both of us well out of reach of whatever was being thrown.

Another of the brothers shouted down to ask the councillor how *he* would respond if the same thing were being done to him. The councillor replied that he himself would not, in any way or form, wish to oppose the march of progress as determined by a democratically elected body, which was, all were agreed (but not the three old men), in the best interests of the borough as a whole. He moved out into the open, smiling, accustomed to applause, and was pelted again.

From inside the house came the sound of hammering. The third brother appeared and said that they had a gun and were not afraid to use it. More policemen and councillors arrived and tapes were strung across the empty street.

Throughout the night, the spotlit house was filled with the sound of the old men singing to a gramophone.

Farouk and I returned in the morning. The crowd of onlookers held placards wishing the old men luck. The councillor said again that he was sure they were going to be reasonable. But this time he said it from inside a police car through a loudspeaker mounted on the roof.

The youngest of the men appeared at the window with tears on his cheeks. He tried to shout out, but was unable to – something about their mother and father. The councillor answered electronically that he fully understood, that every effort was being made, and that as chairman of the Housing Committee he had a responsibility, bestowed upon him as a servant of the borough, to ensure, to the best of his ability –

The rest of his speech was drowned by the booing of the crowd. The old man at the window continued crying.

Farouk and I stood together outside the house all morning and afternoon. Members of the crowd were interviewed by radio and television reporters. Farouk said he wished he had worn something smarter. He asked me if his collar and tie were straight and pushed his way to the front.

A social worker arrived and, after sitting with the councillors for an hour, she repeated in her own jargon precisely what they had already said. Didn't the three old men think they were being just a little bit silly? What would people think of them if they behaved like that? Wouldn't it be the most sensible thing all round if either they came out or let her – she stopped abruptly – let her at least contact the sheltered housing project in which they were to be rehoused? She really did know best. Trust her. They refused to even answer her. There was an hour of silence.

We wanted them to succeed, but I doubt if any of us truly believed they would. They were doing what we should all have done, and that was why we were there to watch.

In the middle of the afternoon the councillor emerged from his car and shouted up that it had become necessary to disconnect the gas and electricity supplies to the house. Mains near by had been fractured and power cables rendered unsafe. It was being done for their own protection. No one regretted it more . . . There was a sharp wind and he stamped his feet. No answer. The social worker left and returned with another.

During the early evening the crowd of onlookers lit fires and sang 'We Shall Not Be Moved', but were, and fell silent as their fires were doused.

Farouk went and I waited alone, waiting for three loud shots. I left an hour later.

The following morning I returned to watch men with hammers and axes smash down the front door as the councillor shouted up his regrets. Throughout the night the temperature had been below freezing. It was out of his hands now, he said. He'd done his best, had wanted to help, fully understood . . . He gave an interview and said it all again. An unavoidable human tragedy. No one knew better than he did how . . . The crowd stood ready to cheer the three old men.

They were led out by the ambulancemen, each with a blanket over his shoulders, small and unsteady; two of them crying, the third looking lost and confused, all three trying to walk like the old soldiers they were. There had been no real preparation, no real supplies beyond a few tins of meat.

The social worker said that everything would sort itself out, that no one would hold what had happened against them. They were to be looked after and cared for like princes. She described to reporters the home to which they would be going. The councillors and police congratulated themselves. The crowd dispersed. Flash bulbs exploded in the half light. A policeman came out of the house carrying an old rifle and two pistols. The reporters asked the councillor if it might all just as easily have ended in tragedy. The councillor, in replying, spelt his name out for the reporters. The street cleared. The ambulance had gone. Furniture from the house was carried out on to the pavement. The circling blue light from the last police car gave everything a strange cinematic look – like an old silent film running at half speed. Faces were caught in it, water and panes of glass. The spotlights were extinguished and everything seemed to become even slower.

I left and walked home.

Farouk asked me what had happened. I told him.

'No suicides?'

No suicides.

He seemed almost disappointed.

Mr Patel said that it had all been very sad. Mrs D wanted to know what they had hoped to achieve by it all. I stopped myself from telling her.

Later, the Irishman said that there had been news of the siege on the radio and that all three brothers had been taken into hospital. I said that it hardly mattered, that it was over.

Later still, Farouk joined the Patels to watch the news report to see if he was on it. He explained to them in detail where we'd been standing.

The tramps are becoming much braver. I have returned home on several occasions to find them sitting on the steps of neighbouring houses. We have been warned against leaving the front door unlocked. Their noise continues to keep me awake at night and I dreamt once of finding them frozen to death on our door steps, their hands and faces black and rigid. I dreamt I was among them and that above us the house was ablaze, a fire in each room, each broken pane of glass heliographing its final destruction. We sat in a frozen circle and held the door firmly shut. We heard the frantic screams of the people inside, but simply laughed at them, congratulating ourselves on what we had done. Only Mrs Patel escaped by leaping through her window and flying through the air like a dolphin rather than a bird, the folds of her sari unwinding behind her until the point at which she disappeared and it fell loose. Her husband watched, shouting after her, surprised and then shocked by the revealed whiteness of her body. He threw their two small children into the street and jumped himself.

It is Christmas Eve. The intermittent snow of the past few days has been dispersed by showers of unseasonally warm rain.

I have taken to leaving my door open and moving freely through the half-empty house, exploring the vacant rooms. An empty room is all that will remain of my own nine years, and then only for a matter of days.

Our water supply has become irregular and the noise of dripping rain is amplified by the empty spaces into which it falls.

I met the Negro in one of the empty rooms and we inspected it together by the light of his torch.

'Shit,' he said, over and over, 'shit shit shit,' at whatever he found. He smashed plates against the walls and kicked the legs of chairs and tables. He asked me what I wanted and I said I wanted the same as him. He said that someone had told him there was money hidden in the house. He asked me if I could imagine finding a hoard of gold and laughed. We sat together in a room that had been empty long before the demolition order and shared one of his cigarettes. When it was between his lips he closed his eyes.

'You write about all this?' he asked, waving his arm around the empty room.

'No.'

'Who want to read about all this anyway?'

'I'll write about you,' I said.

'You do that – you write about me because I am somebody to write about.'

'And her, the girl.'

'She's nothing. Shit.' He took the cigarette and held his head back until it stood vertically from his lips. Ash fell on to his cheek.

'Is she still here?'

'She's here.'

He picked up an ornament of a china fish into which a barometer had been set. He tapped it, and because he had no idea how it worked or what he was supposed to learn from it, he smashed it against the wall. I covered my face but was unable to resist watching through my fingers.

'They smash everything, and we nothing,' he said. He held on to the cigarette. 'We hear you through the floor,' he said.

'And I hear you through the ceiling.'

'No,' he said sharply, as though I had misunderstood him. 'We *hear* you. We hear everyone in the house. We know exactly what they say and doing, you know. Them ought to knock it down now, tonight.' He rubbed his broad hands over the bare floorboards.

'Will the girl go with you?'

'She please herself. She go with *you* if you like.'

'Do you have anywhere to go?'

'When you write that book you have my picture on the front. You have me like this.' He folded his arms and lifted his chin. I told him I would. He showed me the needle marks along his inner forearm. It was because of the girl, he said. I asked him what he meant. He rubbed his fingers and thumb to indicate money. The marks were old and clean. He said they intended moving out of their room into one higher up. I told him there seemed little point. He studied an empty picture frame, breaking it into its four edges and those in half again. The simple act of destruction pleased him and he threw each of the short lengths at the window.

'Africa,' he said suddenly, stopping and watching me.

'Why not?' I would have believed it possible of him once, but not now. He was no different from the rest of us, except that his dreams were probably greater dreams and his disappointments likewise. He repeated the word loudly and heard it fade into the room around us.

There was movement on the landing beneath us. Atlas shouted up for us to identify ourselves. He mistook us for intruders, shouted that the house was still occupied, and left.

The Negro took out a second cigarette, rolled it between his fingers and returned it to his pocket unlit.

We left the room and went up the final short flight of stairs into the empty attic. He kicked the door open. The handle on the inside broke loose and rolled across the boards ahead of us. I heard Mrs D four flights below. He shouted down to her. Then he stood in the middle of the room and jumped heavily up and down until the floor shook and the shattered skylights rattled. He shouted that he was sick of waiting and that he would demolish the house himself. I said I believed him, but he was too preoccupied with his noise making to hear me.

When he stopped the room continued moving.

I left him and went down alone, passing Farouk and Atlas on the third landing. Atlas said he'd suspected it might be me. I said the house was haunted and that the noise had come and gone of its own accord. He said 'Typical', and went into his room. Above us the Negro began jumping again. Farouk showed me a newspaper in which he'd ringed adverts in the Situations Vacant column. I asked him if he'd had any luck so far. He said he hadn't, but that it was only a matter of time. I offered to help him apply. He thanked me formally and went into his room. Above me the Negro went on jumping. I saw the house flattened around us and the girl embarrassed by his actions.

Tomorrow it would be Christmas, and it seemed to me then that no one had even realized.

We spent the afternoon of Christmas day in Mrs D's. I went down with Mr and Mrs Patel, who presented themselves to me an hour early, both smartly dressed and both carrying bottles – Mr Patel the same clear bitter drink we had shared to toast his wife's pregnancy, and Mrs Patel a bottle of peppermint cordial wrapped in tissue paper. He asked me if I thought it was enough. He had oiled and smoothed his hair until it looked like the head of a seal. He said they were early and confessed to being nervous. Mrs Patel said something for him to interpret.

'She wishes you a Very Merry Christmas and Season's Greetings.'

His wife smiled broadly as he spoke.

I asked him how to return the compliment in their own language. He told me. I tried it.

'Merry Chrumas,' she said, repeating it to herself. He watched her proudly, looking from her face to her stomach, where still nothing showed. She had painted her eyes and wore a tight embroidered waistcoat over her sari. I said they both looked very smart and he put his arm round her shoulders as though they were about to have their photograph taken.

At the appointed time we went down to Mrs D's. They presented their bottles. She took Mr Patel's, held it close to her face and said she expected it was very nice. She unwrapped the peppermint and looked surprised. The Irishman stood beside her holding a tumbler of whisky.

'He's hung balls on the tree,' Mrs D whispered to me. 'For Christ's sake notice them.' He had also positioned a naked bulb behind the tree to add to the effect. This cast an elongated shadow over the ceiling and made it look taller.

When we all had drinks we touched glasses and wished each other Merry Christmas. We were a small, exclusive group, and felt it. Mrs D put a finger into her glass and sucked it. Mr Patel drained his clear liquid in a single gulp and stood blinking until the effect wore off.

Farouk arrived a few minutes later. Atlas had been invited and would arrive mid-afternoon. The Negro and his girl had not been invited. Having told us this, Mrs D then went on to say that they would be more than welcome if they did arrive. I said I doubted if they would come. That, she said, was why she hadn't invited them.

Even by his own standards, Farouk was spectacularly dressed. He wore cream-coloured trousers and a cream- and coffee-coloured jacket, tan boots with a prominent buckle, and a shining purple shirt open to the hairs on his chest, through which his medallion rose like the moon through clouds. From his breast pocket hung too much of a red handkerchief. He handed Mrs D a bottle of wine and then presented her with a small bottle of cologne. She showed it to everyone and allowed Farouk to kiss the back of her hand, after which they both became embarrassed and avoided each other.

'Much the same these Ay-rabs,' the Irishman whispered to me. I agreed with him and he refilled my glass from the bottle he held by his side. We – he and I – I realized, formed an even smaller, even more exclusive group.

Farouk and the Patels admired each other's clothes. Mrs D watched them, turned to us and raised her eyebrows.

The Irishman turned on the radio and we listened to the Queen's speech. When she had finished there were tears in his eyes and he re-tuned the radio until carols filled the room. He dabbed at his eyes unashamedly.

'Biggest load of bollocks every year,' he said. 'But the people back home will be listening. I'll be hearing exactly the same as them at exactly the same time.' He raised his glass to the radio. Mrs D interrupted us to ask what we were doing. She saw the Irishman's face and completely misunderstood. She slid her arm through his and prevented him from toasting his abandoned wife and children.

'The Queen's speech,' I said.

'Beautiful,' she said. 'She does a beautiful speech. We were both girls when it started.' She asked me if I knew what Mr Patel was drinking and said he was on his fourth glass.

'They're only small glasses,' I said in his defence.

'They're the ones you've got to watch,' the Irishman said in his own, and refilled our glasses to the brim. Mrs D said she was pleased we were enjoying ourselves.

Excluded from the conversation, Mrs Patel spent most of her time gazing absently around the room, looking at the walls where the pictures had been removed, and at the patches of discoloured carpet where what remained of the furniture had been rearranged. She pointed to the tree, said 'Merry Chrumas', and held up her glass of peppermint, which she drank undiluted.

Mrs D said 'Yes, dear', twice.

'You don't get the feelings yourself, then?' the Irishman asked me, already shaking his head in expectation of my answer.

'Homesickness?'

'That's the one. Homesickness. At Christmas.'

I told him I didn't.

'Ah, it's not the same though, is it?'

'You could have gone back,' I suggested.

He sucked in his cheeks. 'Ah, no, now there I couldn't. But I suppose if you have a family, then Christmas is the time to take advantage of them.' He shook his head at the thought.

I left him and stood with Mrs D. From her small kitchen came the smell of cooked meat and apples. I asked if she'd enjoyed her Christmas dinner. She said she hadn't. 'Pork,' she whispered, pulled a face and rubbed her stomach.

'You had it with –' I nodded over my shoulder.

'It's a delight watching him eat,' she said.

'I can imagine.' My own dinner had consisted of an individual pudding in a tin which had taken two hours to cook and had not been worth it.

'It's nice to make the effort.'

I knew then that for all of us that was precisely what Christmas had been reduced to – an effort. Without the Queen's speech it might never have existed at all.

The Irishman sat in a chair beside the tree and started to sing. The glass balls spun and cast patterns of coloured light over his face and arms. Mrs Patel clapped.

'Thank you, madam.' He started up again.

'He's got a fine singing voice,' Mrs D said. She closed her eyes and hummed an approximation of his tune. It was this, rather than the Irishman's singing, which silenced us all.

A few minutes later, Atlas arrived. Mrs D informed him that he'd missed the Queen's speech. She asked him what he wanted to drink and he said he'd stick with what he'd brought. The Irishman said something about never trusting a man who drank only his own drink.

Ensuring that all our glasses were full, Mrs D announced that she wished to propose a toast. 'To us,' she said. 'To us all.' It was inevitable. We drank and hoped it would be all she had to say. It wasn't.

'It's been a good house,' she said.

'A good house,' the Irishman repeated, draining his glass and wiping at the shapes of light moving across his chest.

'You haven't all been here as long as I have.' She closed her eyes.

'That's a fact,' the Irishman said.

She ignored him. 'We've had some good times.'

We each tried to think of them.

'Good times, bad times.' Now she was maudlin and looked about to cry.

'We've all had bad times,' the Irishman said.

She cried.

The Irishman got up to comfort her. He looked around to see who had offended her, and then almost fell with her back into his chair. He spoke to her softly and pressed her head into his shoulder. We stood around them with our glasses held ready. Unexpectedly, Mrs Patel also began to cry. Mr Patel tried to tell us that she was overcome with emotion, but the words came out slurred and with letters misplaced. Farouk, Atlas and I looked on, excluded.

'Always too much crying,' Farouk said dismissively.

'She's depressed,' I suggested to the Irishman.

'She's pissed off,' he answered back. 'Same thing, I suppose.'

'She shouldn't have bothered,' I said. Everyone agreed.

'Upsetting herself,' Farouk said.

I turned up the radio and with the noise of the carols the situation was eased.

The Irishman tried to dance and almost fell over.

'Drunk,' Atlas said, unnecessarily.

Farouk asked if there was any food, and rather than refuse him, Mrs D pretended not to have heard. The carols were followed by hymns.

Later still a Salvation Army band marched along a neighbouring street. We were silenced and urged to the window to listen. Mrs D said that the band always came. The Irishman wondered aloud why they bothered. We waited for the musicians to appear. When the music faded we returned disappointed to the centre of the room.

'They used to come down here,' she said.

'*Used* to,' the Irishman echoed.

After that she began to drink more rapidly, mixing what remained in the bottles around the room.

By the time the rest of us left, the Irishman was asleep, his feet stretched to the fire. Mrs D saw us out, kissed Atlas, Farouk and myself, and shook Mrs Patel's hand. Mr Patel himself stood out of reach. She closed the door on us and began to sing. We heard her as we climbed the stairs, her voice rising until it filled the stairwell, and then silent as she drank, unable to resume.

Lynette emerged from the bedroom wearing a lime-green trouser suit and carrying the two vanity cases she took with her to every show – one for herself and one for the dogs. It was Friday; she would be away for the whole weekend, returning Monday afternoon. She was staying at a small commercial hotel and I was to remain in charge of the kennels until her return. Her mother would not come because by then things between us had deteriorated to the point where we could tolerate only the other's absence. The kennel-maids would return the following morning, but on Sunday the care of the dogs would be entirely in my hands. Lynette explained all this as I followed her through the house. At the door she kissed me coldly and said that she trusted me. The kiss was for the benefit of the neighbours, her declaration of trust a warning.

I said, 'What could possibly go wrong?' and felt like a child shouting back at a bully from a position well out of reach. I stood at the kerb and watched her leave.

The two kennel-maids sat in the kitchen. When I told them she'd gone they both let out a mouthful of smoke with a long sigh of relief. The younger girl was still uncertain of how much she should say about Lynette in my presence. The older one said, 'Thank God for that.'

By then the kennels extended the full length of the garden and ran into a compound fenced off from the land beyond. For Lynette and myself it was to be our last weekend together, and we spent it apart.

I went out for a drink. When I returned mid-afternoon the two girls were still in the kitchen, smoking and drinking tea. I joined them and asked if the dogs had been all right. The younger one said she supposed so. The other said that the smell from the kennels made her sick. I asked her why she continued to work there. 'Money,' she said. All three of us seemed somehow defeated by Lynette's absence, and by what we were supposed to be doing, but weren't.

When the younger girl had gone outside, the older one moved into the seat beside me and told me she was looking for another job.

The younger girl returned with a white poodle cradled in her arms and said it had been sick. We were undecided what to do. The girl thought it should stay in the house, where at least it was warm. I agreed and she settled the dog into a cardboard box beside the central heating boiler. After that we forgot about it and returned to our conversation.

An hour later the poodle was sick again, bringing up a small pool of viscous saliva. The older girl said that if I wanted her to come back the following day, then she would. I told her I could manage. The younger girl said I ought to call the vet if the poodle was sick again. I said that I would.

When they'd gone I went into my own small room and inspected the sheets of typing beside the typewriter. I read a few pages and they satisfied me. I hadn't done any real work for the past six months.

Downstairs, the sick poodle had left its box and was scratching at the door into the living room. I kicked it away and turned out the light.

I sat with a bottle and watched television all evening. I fell asleep twice and then remained awake until three in the morning. The bottle was almost empty.

It was midday when I woke and the room around me stank. Against the door and wall I saw the splatter of diarrhoea and several pools of vomit. The dog had somehow followed me upstairs and been shut in the bedroom with me. I heard it whimpering under the bed. I called to it softly, and when it emerged I grabbed it and threw it against the door. It fell to the floor, shook itself and ran back under the bed, where it lay shaking. I went into the bathroom and heard it run downstairs.

I dressed and went down after it. It was sitting in the box by the boiler watching me calmly, as though the flimsy cardboard created a shield, behind which it was safe. I picked it up by the scruff of its neck and dropped it outside into one of the holding compounds. I swore at it again, and then at the others as they began howling for food.

In the kitchen I cooked and ate a large breakfast and then went through the house looking for other signs of the dog's illness. I found none.

In the afternoon the older girl returned and admitted that the dogs hadn't been fed the previous afternoon. She saw the empty box and asked about the poodle. I said it had recovered. She cleaned the kitchen while I fed the dogs. After that we went out for a drink followed by a drive into the country. We stopped for an hour at an empty picnic site, and afterwards, as she made up her face in the rear-view mirror, she said she'd decided to hand in her notice.

When we returned home in the late afternoon the poodle was dead. It lay with its mouth and eyes open, and with a pool of the same clear vomit around its head.

The girl said 'Oh fuck' – more at what was likely to happen upon Lynette's return than at the death itself. I found myself unable to feel anything for the dead dog. All I could think about was concocting a story to tell Lynette. I removed the dog's collar and identification. The girl said I ought to wear gloves. Looking from her to the dog I felt suddenly exposed and knew that I was about to be punished for what we had done, what I had allowed to happen.

I put the dog in a large plastic bag, bound it with Sellotape, and awaited Lynette's inevitable call.

She rang at seven, successful. I tried to sound pleased. She told me about the hotel. In the silence I could sense that she knew something was wrong and that she wasn't asking for fear of being told.

'Everything all right at the kennels?'

'Fine. Everything's fine.'

'And the dogs?'

I killed one. It was sick and I kicked it around the house and killed it. 'The dogs are fine. One of the poodles seemed a bit under the weather so I brought him indoors.' I realized then that I didn't even know the dog's sex.

'Which one?'

I read the name on the tag in my hand.

'And?'

'He was sick in the bedroom.'

'*She* was sick in the bedroom.'

'Sorry, yes, she was –'

'And since?'

'Fine. She's here now . . .' I held the receiver to the open door and the noise of the other dogs.

'Have you called the vet?'

'Yes, this afternoon.'

'Keep her indoors, away from the others.' I heard the clicking sound she made when she was thinking. She told me what time she would be home and hung up.

I rang the vet. He asked me how the dog appeared and I told him it seemed to have recovered. He told me to keep it warm and away from the others. He would come in the morning. I hung up, relieved, pleased with myself, as though I had successfully solved the problem and, having solved it, the dog would now somehow miraculously revive. When Lynette got back I would say the dog had just died. I would take it out of the plastic bag and arrange it in the box beside the boiler. The stains in the bedroom would remain as the evidence of its sickness and my concern.

I spent the remainder of the day cleaning out the kennels. I went indoors only when it grew dark and the dogs were quiet.

But the vet would examine the dog and know precisely how long it had been dead. Everything would come out. The girl would deliver her version of the story to protect herself and Lynette would want to know why she had come to the house on a Sunday. Around me the silver cups and trophies cast back my distorted reflection. The long names of dogs and their achievements were engraved across my cheeks, and the insuppressible guilt was in my eyes for anyone to see.

The following day Lynette arrived early, before I'd called the vet. She took the dog from the box, and without speaking to me, carried it outside. Stopping between the lines of excited dogs, she turned and accused me of lying.

'*Lying*?' I tried to sound indignant. 'Ask the vet.'

'I did. I rang him as soon as I hung up yesterday. You called him ten minutes later. He rang me back.'

The younger girl appeared in the yard behind us. She saw the dead dog and began to cry. 'It was sick,' she said. 'We brought it in.'

Lynette continued staring at me, as though the girl didn't exist. 'You lied,' she said. It was the precise moment of our separation. I left them both and went indoors.

The older girl didn't turn up for work. Her parents rang to apologize. Lynette said she was fired and they became indignant. She hung up on them. Only then did I fully understand the finality of the point at which we had arrived and the inevitability of our journey towards it. She wrapped the dog in a blanket and held it in her lap. She began to cry. She was still crying when I left an hour later.

I went without saying anything, and once outside I could not rid myself of the impression that what we had just done to each other had been acted out by two entirely different people, elsewhere, over something completely different, and that she and I were not in the least involved or to blame for what had happened.

I slept and woke and dreamed. I saw my parents and the guests at our wedding, saw them shaking their heads at me and sitting with small dogs in their laps. I saw Mrs D pull a face of disgust as Lynette introduced herself and thrust one of the dogs into her arms. The others – the Patels, Atlas, Farouk and the Irishman – stood around me. The Negro gave his girl to me and I was afraid to touch her. The Irishman encouraged me, but when I brought her into my room it was cold and dark and she complained. Lynette was sitting on the bed saying over and over that she had known all along. The dogs were arranged in a circle at her feet. Atlas materialized and stood beside the girl, naked. She caressed him and said things about me which made him laugh and her smile cruelly. By the time they had faded, the girl was undressed and spreadeagled on the bed. Mrs Patel stood beside her and pointed to parts of her own body.

It was almost midnight when I awoke and our celebrations seemed to have taken place days rather than hours ago. I heard men singing outside, stopping and starting abruptly as they encouraged each other to continue. There was a light beneath my door, and a pale square cast upwards from the street. I heard Farouk and Atlas on the landing. Beneath me I half heard Mrs D and the Irishman, laughing, shouting occasionally, the rattle of their glasses and the noise of a television musical which filled the house. I lay without moving, listening to it all.

When I eventually did fall back to sleep I dreamt that the house was being pulled down around me and that I remained precariously perched in my bed on a half-missing floor and that everyone else was down in the street, pointing up at me and laughing. Even the tramps had joined in and were being encouraged by the Irishman, with whom they shared their drink. Farouk and Mr Patel held one of Farouk's colourful jackets between them and were imploring me to jump and save myself. 'Save myself from what?' I shouted down. They couldn't answer. Farouk took back his jacket. The others turned away, disappointed.

The tramps dispersed over the derelict land, taking the Irishman with them. Mrs D tried to tempt him back by waving glossy photographs of her new home at him. The old Chinese woman's funeral parted the crowd and everyone fell into a respectful silence with their heads bowed and hands crossed. I shouted down to them but no one looked up. Lynette returned in a chauffeur-driven car and said again that she had known all along how it would end. Behind her the mural was once again complete. I stood in the middle of it, ten feet high, waving a flag; people marched in a group behind me.

The house was demolished until only its strongest walls remained standing. I was suspended in mid-air, knowing that the slightest movement would throw me down and bury me. When the cortège had passed only Mr Patel looked up. I tried to shout to him, but he waved me away and turned to his wife. Atlas was comforting Mrs D at the destruction of her home and the disappearance of the Irishman. It was too dark to see far beyond them and I was still too frightened to try and move. I raised my arms to plead. The bed shifted and I fell.

It was four in the morning and the house was cold and silent. Beyond the darkened streets below, the sky still glowed above the distant city. I felt the way I used to feel upon waking during the first few weeks after my arrival – expecting something to happen, but knowing that nothing would. We had ten days left in the house. There were no longer any certainties. I felt empty, and devoid of all expectation and hope for the future.

On the day following Boxing Day the Negro and his girl simply went out and never came back. When it became clear that they had gone for good, I went with Mrs D into their small room. It looked as cramped and as sparse as it had done prior to their arrival. There was no trace of them ever having been there. Mrs D searched but found nothing. Refusing to be defeated, she took a deep breath and said 'There!' I was instructed to do the same. A faint scent remained. I asked her what it proved.

Later in the day Farouk went out with several of his plastic-covered jackets and returned without them.

The decorations were still up in the hallway and the television continued to show and repeat festive programmes. Christmas was still there for any of us bothered to make the effort to retrieve it. None of us did.

The Irishman and Mrs D stand in the corridor leading to her room and argue. He is leaving. He stands with his feet on either side of his bag of tools. He is taking with him no more nor less than what he arrived with. Her anger is little more than another reflex, brought on by the acceleration of events around her and because, despite all her preparations, she remains unprepared. Her furniture might have gone ahead of her, but everything else remains firmly fixed in the past. She calls him the Final Straw. He says he can't deny it and wishes it were otherwise. She asks him where he intends going. He says he has fewer expectations than the rest of us. She tries to tempt him with the promise of a meal. A farewell meal. He owes her that much at least. He stops answering her. She says she's seen him in the bars with other women. He says he wishes it hadn't come to this, straightens his cap the way he always straightens it before going out and leaves.

I'd seen him earlier. He said he was going down to see her. I wished him well and he understood it to mean with her.

'You'll be going yourself soon,' he said.

I told him I would. There was nothing any of us could say to each other that didn't end painfully.

'She'll be upset, you think?'

'She must have expected it.'

He took from his bag a pint of milk and a packet of cooked meat and put them on my table.

'Women!' she shouted after him as he went. 'Other bloody women!'

Perhaps she needed it to let him go. He picked up his bag of tools and went.

She waited for ten minutes and then stood at the bottom of the stairs shouting his name.

When I saw her later in the day she asked me if I'd seen him. I said I hadn't. She said he'd probably be in a bar somewhere. She complained that he was unreliable and that he was supposed to be having a meal with her. I asked her what they were having. She said it was a surprise. Her mother had been a marvellous cook. Things like that were never lost. She took a deep breath and smiled. I said I was sure that whatever it was would be delicious. She said you could tell just from the smell.

The Irishman had not gone very far. I saw him the following day in one of the bars he frequented. He said he'd found another room. I told him what Mrs D had said about the meal and he left me at the first opportunity and went back to the men with whom he'd been sitting upon my arrival.

She stopped me in the hallway upon my return home. She wanted me to accompany her into the Irishman's room just as I had done with the Negro's.

In the evening I packed my own belongings. The process lasted less than an hour and the boxes of books were too heavy to lift. I unpacked and rearranged everything. There were marks in the dust to indicate precisely where everything had been.

Atlas went on New Year's Day. The same men who had helped him in with his belongings arrived to help him out with them. It was as inevitable as Mrs D's Christmas speech that he would knock and say his farewells. Mr and Mrs Patel and Farouk shook his hand. I wished he'd just disappeared like the West Indians or the Negro and his girl. The Patels wanted to know how close to the house his transport had been able to get. For three consecutive days they have prepared and waited for the van to arrive and take them and their belongings to that flat above the shop. Atlas described his new home, its furnishings, surroundings, views. Mrs Patel cradled her unborn child in her hands and wanted to be able to speak as enthusiastically of their own. Instead she cried. Atlas said it had all been too much for her. Farouk agreed. 'Such sweet sorrow,' Atlas said. I told him that his friends were waiting for him. He said it was the least of what was waiting for him. I wanted to challenge him and ask him why he'd bothered knocking if it was only to do this to us.

The following day the vagrants began to leave the waste ground and empty houses. They left singly and in small groups, walking purposefully over the open ground in almost straight lines, as though certain of their destination, of the point at which they would converge and begin again. I watched them go from my window.

In the night I heard Mrs D shout the Irishman's name. I might have heard it, she might have shouted it, or it might simply have been part of my own dreaming sleep. And if she had called it then it might still have been no more than part of a dream of her own.

Two days after the departure of Atlas, the Patels have finally gone. Their van arrived unexpectedly and I saw Mr Patel outside in the light snow with his pyjama jacket tucked into his trousers, and with only his slippers on his feet. The man in the van – a friend of his brother-in-law – argued with him and seemed reluctant to leave his cab and help with the loading of their belongings.

Mrs D came out to see them off. Mr Patel tried to explain how he felt about what was happening. I told him we knew and he said he would miss us. Mrs Patel was anxious for them to leave and her urgency embarrassed him. Mrs D said it was all too much for her, and left us. The shop, it seems, is to be demolished in eighteen months' time. The driver of the van sat with his fist on the horn. Mr Patel climbed in. I shook his hand through the open window and waved until they were out of sight.

Inside, Mrs D had been crying. She said the Patels had been happy with her and waited for my confirmation. She began to reminisce about their arrival. I knew for a fact that she had tried to evict them after the birth of each of the children. She said that what was happening to them was a shame after having come so far. I wanted to ask her how far she thought any of us had come in the past nine years. I left her and neither saw nor heard anything of her for the rest of the day.

Farouk returned later in the afternoon and left again shortly afterwards with more of his clothes. Neither of us spoke. I wondered how many of his jackets and perfectly creased trousers still remained. He used the fire escape and, when he saw me, he looked embarrassed and ashamed. Later still, I heard him singing. When his voice is low he manages to sound like two men, when it is high, like a girl. His audience bangs on walls and shouts at him through empty rooms. The slightest sound reverberates.

I expected Mr Patel to return under the pretext of looking for something he had forgotten or returning something he had taken by mistake, but he never came and I never saw him again.

Today is our last day in the house, tonight our last night. Mrs D has avoided me. She expects sirens. I expect to find her beneath a table, shouting her warnings. Proud Stand by Defiant Resident. We have never understood her. She seems confused about who has gone and who remains. She and I are alone. The street has finally been closed to all traffic. I Shall Not Be Moved Says . . . Last night was cloudless and bright, and I piled empty boxes against my window to shut out the glare of the moon. Our electricity supply is shortly to be disconnected. One Woman's Fight. There are noises in the house where previously there has been only silence.

A water pipe has burst and the street is covered with a sheet of ice which advances and retreats each day. It is all the evidence she needs. She made up her face and dressed as though she were about to go out, but she went no further than the cluttered back garden, where she examined what people had thrown out. She said she would never forgive the West Indians and seemed to think that the Irishman was shortly to return.

I slept in the afternoon and awoke to the sound of cats fighting in the empty houses. Our electricity had gone and the smell of burning candles filled the house.

More snow has been forecast. Days ago, she said that to see the house destroyed would kill her. Either that or she would Die of Grief.

The women on the poster are still there, their lips still pursed like the fixed mouth of the speared fish, their eyes still vividly white.

Mrs D spoke to her husbands. They told her what she wanted to hear. She took them down, kissed them and packed them between her softest clothes.

She stopped me and demanded to know why we'd let this happen to her. She'd worked like a black to make the house what it was. I said I didn't think she could say that – Didn't I believe her? – any longer. Working like a black, I said. I was deaf. Ask anyone. She supposed smugly that knowing about these things made them right. She went back to the war. For Peace of Mind, she said. Her mother went back further. God rest her soul. Small mercy that *she* wasn't alive to see all this. It would have killed her too. Ten years the blacks had been there, twenty. The conversation continued after I'd gone. She shouted up to me. I said, 'Looking for me, Mrs D?' But she wouldn't have heard.

I awoke from the dreamless sleep and looked down over the garden. She was still there. Her husbands had laid a lawn and planted displays of brightly coloured flowers. They stood in their shirt sleeves and dug to prove their devotion. There had never been two finer men. She tapped powdery soil from empty margarine cartons, the contents of which had grown only to die of neglect.

The machinery of our destruction stands around us sheeted with yellow tarpaulins.

She listened to her radio until the batteries ran down. As one signal grew weak so she found a stronger one.

There were traffic jams, a royal visit, a hundredth birthday, storm warnings, the threat of hostilities, another traffic jam, cinema showings. It was all happening. It was always colder somewhere else.

In the darkness the tarpaulins appeared almost luminescent.

Reports of wind-driven snow drifts ten-feet deep, foreign voices, hostilities, chamber music, military bands.

Here there is no wind or snow. A noise from the Patels' empty room sounds like the wailing in the dream. There is no rain and no cloud. The sky above the levelled land is almost colourless and blinding.

Tell her she couldn't call them 'Blacks'. Where was the justice in it? She had been promised an ornamental pool by Number One, somewhere to sit. By Number Two a greenhouse for tomatoes. It had always been a good garden for the sun. And soil. I wouldn't have understood. She asked me what I thought of the Irishman. She wanted to tell me about the Other Women. Her Other Men counted for less than the drinks they bought her. It was what she wanted clearly understood. She might as well be dead already for all the difference it would make.

After the traffic jams came explosions, a murder, warnings of rough seas, hijacked aircraft, talking chimpanzees, failed rockets, broadcasts to shipping a thousand miles away.

I went from my room to the top of the house, and from there back down to the bottom.

An hour later she ran in screaming from the garden, slammed the door and stood with one hand against her chest, the other covering her mouth. I asked her what was wrong and she said she'd seen a rat. I told her that it was nothing for her to worry about. A rat as big as a cat, she said. A dog. With teeth. She spread her hands to indicate the size of the rat and afterwards spoke of it almost proudly as the beginning of the end.